M

Boo Riley

God bless!

David E. Arp

aka Boo Riley

This is a work of fiction. Names, characters, places, and incidents either are the product of the author's imagination or are used fictitiously, and any resemblance to actual persons living or dead, business establishments, events, or locales, is entirely coincidental.

Me and Jake
COPYRIGHT 2018 by Boo Riley

Contact Information: titleadmin@pelicanbookgroup.com

Scripture quotations, unless otherwise indicated are taken from the King James translation, public domain.

Cover Art by *Artist Nicola Martinez*

Watershed Books, a division of Pelican Ventures, LLC
www.pelicanbookgroup.com PO Box 1738 *Aztec, NM * 87410

Watershed Books praise and splash logo is a trademark of Pelican Ventures, LLC

Publishing History
First Watershed Edition, 2018
Paperback Edition ISBN 978-1-5223-0017-5
Electronic Edition ISBN 978-1-5223-0015-1
Published in the United States of America

Dedication

To Anthony, Floyd, and children like them. To Jesus,
Who hears their cries.

1

The rattle of Dad's old pickup lingered long after the taillights disappeared into the darkness. Cameron stared after it. I stared after it. I'd heard twins think alike, and it must have been true because there we stood, like statues in the cool morning.

A pair of goats had more sense.

I let my right hand rest on Jake's head. My one-eyed Black and Tan Coonhound was never far from me. "What now?" I asked. Like I didn't already know the answer.

"What time is it?" my brother whispered.

I shrugged. He knew I didn't own a watch, but he asked anyway. "Morning time. Real early, I think, but maybe not. Clouds might be hiding the first rays. No stars out and all. Why are you whispering?"

Cameron let out a hard breath and looked up at the black sky. "I don't want to wake up. We got to bed just shy of eleven. I don't feel like I slept an hour before Dad yelled at us. I wonder what's stuck in his craw. Did you hear anything he said to Momma Ray before we left? I didn't."

Our stepmom demanded we call her Momma Ray. "I heard 'em talking, but all lovey-dovey, with Dad sipping coffee between times. They sound like a tractor tire hissing air around a nail, whispering back and forth at each other. You know they don't have us in mind when they do all that mushy stuff."

"Yeah, you're right."

"Let's get cranked up and cut some hay."

"Um, wait. What's that noise? T, I think your angel is on the run?"

Everyone called me Ty but my brother. I liked it that way.

I looked down to my right, then behind us. What in the world? Jake had slipped out from under my hand and walked away without me knowing. "Jake *is* an angel. Only looks like a dog."

"Brother, we're fourteen, nearly fifteen. Angels and coon dogs? Come on. That's fairytale stuff."

"Well, how do you explain—?"

"I don't have to. I'm not the one who thinks an old flop-eared hound's an angel."

My beliefs about Jake were an ongoing subject Cameron wouldn't let be. Cameron's anger was quick to flare up. He was lucky I wasn't like him. His nose would've been bloody about then.

A deep bay echoed across the hayfield. Jake knew I was looking for him and hollered to let me know what he was up to.

Cameron elbowed me. "T, I'll bet Jake's on a coon. Let's go!"

Just because a coonhound has *coon* in his name doesn't mean he's limited to chasing only masked bandits. Given the chance, Jake was apt to go after any critter that had legs to run on. Rabbits, squirrels, deer, bobcats and even a stray housecat could attract his attention.

Most times, I'd be the first one to run off and chase critters with Jake, but...Dad would show up again soon, sure as shooting, and he'd know by looking at the field we'd been playing around instead of tending to his business. "What about mowing? Dad said—"

"You didn't listen. Dad said to cut hay when the sun comes up. The sun ain't up. I'm taking him at his word. Let's have some fun for once."

Cameron made a lot of sense.

I hoped Jake hadn't jumped a deer. They don't tree. They keep running and running and running.

Jake could howl the bark off an oak tree when he got to going and made it easy to follow his line of travel. His bark led us across the pasture.

The sun was closer to coming up than I thought. Before we entered the trees at a run, I could see good enough to avoid low limbs, rocks, and tree trunks. And it was cloudy. Low and wispy, like fog, only higher, the kind Dad always said would burn off as soon as the sun came up.

The ridge across the north side of our pasture rose to our front. I pointed left, cut right, and yelled back at Cameron. "Go that way. I'll circle in case they cross the top. Meet me at the pond."

Cameron and I knew the country around our pasture. We had explored the woods with Jake many times. If I could make the top of the ridge before Jake chased his prey up the hill, I could call him off.

We didn't own a gun, so we chased coons just to hear Jake's voice. Maybe, too, we liked to run for the fun of it, free of the everyday chores that took up all of our time. If the coon treed, Jake would give him a good what-for, howling out of frustration because the chase was over, and we could get back to the hayfield and go to work.

My heartbeat kept pace with my feet as I pounded up the steep ground between rocks and trees. Bushes and tall grass shed the morning dew and soaked my britches. Once on top, I stopped to catch my breath and listen to Jake's ramblings below. The coon was leading him in a circle. Jake's bark echoed in the cool morning air and sounded like two dogs on the hunt.

Then, the biggest ruckus broke loose. Screaming and howling the likes I never heard before erupted. The hair jumped up on my head and goose bumps popped out on me from head to toe. What in the world? It sounded like Jake caught the boogieman. I headed back down the hill as fast as I could run.

The pond wasn't big. About fifty paces across. Cameron and I had visited the little water hole many times for a drink when we could escape the hayfield without Dad catching us. Sometimes the water was clear, most times not. The smell of mud, rotten plants, and frogs and such made me wonder how I'd put my lips in it for a long drink so many times before.

The woods opened up and the pond came into view. Jake swam around in the middle, like he couldn't make up his mind which way to go. A big coon scurried out of the water and disappeared into the bushes on the opposite bank. To Jake's left, another critter thrashed in the water. A red and white...what? Coon? I stopped and stared, stuck in the mud like a dead tree stump. Moron.

Cameron wore a red ball cap and a white shirt, but he couldn't swim.

My scream propelled me into the water.

2

The cool morning turned into a day hot enough to pop the corn on the stalk. I couldn't tell if my clothes were still wet from saving Cameron's hide or from the buckets of sweat pouring out of me.

I looked back at my brother for the hundredth time. Made me want to poke him on the nose again. Acted like Mr. Cool and nothing had happened. Said he saved Jake from drowning. Said the coon was perched on his head, hanging onto his ears and riding him like a horse. Bunch of boloney. I knew better. He might have helped Jake, but he about drowned himself and wouldn't admit it. He spit out green water, moss, and mud for five minutes. I didn't see one pop out, but he might have swallowed a frog too.

The thought of losing him wasn't something I could ponder without a knot forming in my throat.

Jake lay stretched out in the shade of a red oak. Bees buzzing around his face couldn't stir a twitch out of him. He had a nose for coons. That's how he lost his eye. One night, we chased a wily old bandit through the woods on the backside of the house and he ran into a tree or a bush. I didn't see exactly what happened, but I heard him yelp. He pawed at his face, but never shed a tear.

I cried for him.

The poor guy has been lopsided ever since. Turns to the right so he doesn't bump into things, walks with his head tilted left, and lies on the bad eye, the left side, where it used to be, so he can see me.

He looked like he slept now, sprawled out in the cool shade, but I knew he watched. He saw everything. Jake was my angel. Not one of those angels who protected me with a sword or could carry me away on swift wings. I'd heard tell of that kind before. Jake was a watcher, a witness, and someday, he'll tell folks what happened to me and Cameron, tell them about our childhood.

Cameron said I'm dumb, but I don't care. Jake keeps an eye out for danger, like snakes and rats and the like. And he tells me when Dad's coming. Only an angel would know about our Dad's coming and goings and that's a fact.

Aphids and grasshoppers fled before the tractor. The bugs didn't like hot afternoons. They were napping. I'd like to have been, what, where, I don't know, napping in the grass with the bugs or laying in the shade with Jake.

Steering the old tractor around and around the field numbed my mind. Engine noise numbed my hearing. Vibration numbed my feet until they felt like they didn't belong to me.

A bump rocked the tractor and my heart bounced off the roof of my mouth. Before I could push in the clutch and hit the brakes, the three-point hitch on the back shook like a dog shedding water.

Sometimes I could have just kicked myself. I knew better. Daydreaming, floating off into my own world. Something bad happened every time. Probably clipped a rock and when I looked back, sure enough, there it lay, a white one the size of a cantaloupe. Done some damage somewhere sure as shooting. I raised the sickle mower and examined it for broken teeth, but didn't see one missing.

When I hopped down with two adjustable wrenches, Jake raised his head and then let it fall back onto the grass like the effort was too much for him. He'd seen this before and knew his help wouldn't be needed.

Cameron gave me a look, something between a frown and a pained look, and crawled down from his tractor. "T, you hit a rock, didn't you? You need to watch what you're doing. Dad is going to show up. He always does when something breaks."

My brother took big steps through the deep grass. With every stride, his knobby knees poked through large holes in his jeans. Only his sunburned ears kept the tattered red ball cap from sliding down over his eyes. Looked like he dried out from the swim he took. His shirt flapped in the breeze.

It was a waste of time to argue, though Cameron didn't think so, and looking at him set his tongue to wagging again. "You can't sit up there on the seat with your head in the clouds. You ain't that high up. Got to look where you're going, not just put the tractor in gear and drive like a kid on an outing for a soda pop with a pretty girl."

"Cameron, you know who you sound like? If you'll shut up and help me, Dad won't know. And since you mentioned it—what would you know about outings of any kind? Or pretty girls for that matter? You don't even like girls. We can't even drive yet." I went to work removing the bolts.

"I can drive a tractor, and I don't have to shut up. I know plenty about girls and such too. Just never been for a soda pop with one. You're so smart…we could walk to the soda shop."

The bolts came loose easy. Wasn't like they were rusty, and it hadn't been long since I'd clipped a rock. I'd hit one the last time I cut hay. "You're the one who's arguing about nothing, stating the obvious. I know Dad might come. I know I hit a rock. Pretty girls don't have nothing to do with sitting on a tractor. Quit bumping your gums and pull out the blade. I'll have it fixed in a jiffy."

"I don't bump my gums when I talk. I got teeth." He bared and snapped them together as proof.

"Cameron, please, bend over and pull, so I can watch *these* teeth. Be quiet."

"OK, watch your fingers."

"I'm watching. Get on with it."

Cameron eased the blade of jagged cutters from the guards.

"Stop! There it is." I pointed with the wrench. "The sagging one. Only need to tighten the rivets. Get the rock I hit, right there behind you. I'll use it for backing and beat the rivets with a wrench."

It might have been silly, but I felt good using the same rock that started all the fuss in the first place for a solid base to flatten the rivets, tightening the cutter. It gave me a chance to hit something. Maybe I was more like Cameron than I thought.

Jake abandoned the shade tree with his head high, nose into the hot breeze. A long howl emerged from somewhere down deep in him. As he let it go, he looked like he hung on to the ground with his toenails to keep from flying off into the woods. The lunch whistle at the old sawmill didn't have nothing on Jake.

Something icy moved up my spine, like a warm breeze cooling sweat. My heart jumped back in my throat, stopping up the hole, making it hard to breathe.

Dad's blue Ford pickup appeared seconds later, trailed by a cloud of red dust. A string of tin cans behind newlyweds leaving the white church down the road from the house sounded about the same. Bumps and such didn't slow Dad none.

Jake disappeared into the brush. The engine revved. Dad must have seen we were stopped.

Cameron gave me a stinging slap on the back and whined, "I told you. You never listen. He always comes. Now we can't have a drink and it's your fault."

I put the wrenches in my hip pocket and poked him in the shoulder with my fist. "You don't know we can't have a drink. Besides, I thought you got enough pond water this morning."

"Well, I didn't. And that's different."

"What's different about it?"

"You're trying to change the subject. You watch. Dad is going to beat the fire out of you for hitting the rock, and we're not going to wet a whistle, neither of us."

"You can't whistle anyways. Just get on your tractor and rake hay." I pointed across the pasture. "I'll take the licking."

Cameron's cheeks filled with air. Relief. I'd seen it before. He'd made up his mind. Ten long paces and one jump took him to the seat of the faded green tractor and out of Dad's reach. He didn't crank up and leave, though. He had to see what was going to happen.

Dad turned off the dirt road into the hay pasture without checking his speed. His lips moved. He chewed tobacco, but this didn't have anything to do with chewing.

Something came over me as I watched his chubby cheeks jiggle with every bump. I knew, sure as the sun rises, something was going to happen.

He drove up and stopped. The pickup door opened with the squeak and pop of worn hinges. Dad lumbered out, stretched to just above the doorframe and stuck out his chest, working his tan shirt in around the waist of his jeans. Relaxed, his belly sagged over his belt. He duck-waddled but with his feet splayed out. More penguin in the walk than duck. "I can't leave you boys no time. Just tear things up on purpose, both of you."

I gritted my teeth. No time like the present. "Dad, it's my fault. I clipped a rock. Only loosened a tooth. We already fixed it. I know deep grass is no excuse and I got to pay attention."

Dad's stare bored holes into the part of my soul that would give me up as a liar, pretending to be sorry. If our eyes met, he'd know right off, so I stared at his scuffed boots.

"Dad, can I have a drink?" Cameron broke the silence.

For whatever reason, Dad had a burr in his shorts about letting us drink water.

Cameron wasn't thinking. I told him I'd take the whooping, and I meant it. Dad had been focused on me, but not anymore. Cameron just had to ask.

Dad's face crinkled into something that would make a bear glad he sat on a tractor out of reach. "Do you know where you can get a drink? Go get you one if you do, but don't look in the back of my pickup. That water can is mine!" Tobacco spit dribbled down his chin. A drop or two made it to his shirt. The rest he smeared across the back of his hand.

Cameron cranked up his tractor, put it in gear, and let out the clutch. The rotary-rake attached to the three-point spun, throwing fresh-cut grass into a tall row as he sped by.

Dad grabbed me by the shirt and pulled me to him. The odor of tobacco reached down the back of my throat and threatened to gag me. "Boy, you tend to your business. Get this here mower back together and get to work. I want this field finished by nightfall. Tomorrow, me and you got to run a trotline in the slough. The missus wants some catfish." He pushed me away, to an arm's length, like he held the newspaper so he could see the letters, and then he turned loose.

"Maybe you ought to take Cameron. He likes to fish."

Shucks. I was ready for him to strike, but he still got me with the back of his hand. I don't know why I opened my mouth. I'd almost made it.

Dad pointed a stubby finger in my face. "Don't you try to stare me down, boy. You better find something to look at 'sides me."

My stare moved from the beads of sweat on his pockmarked nose down to a white button on his shirt, next to a slimy smearing of tobacco spit.

He walked to his pickup, put one foot on the doorjamb, then stopped. "That slap was for breaking the mower and costing me time. Your mouth just reminded me I owed you."

3

How in the world does the sun get so high so quick and then take forever to fall? Momma Ray said a watched pot never boils. Well, a watched sun never sets either.

Plenty of time to ponder the sun's movements for the latter half of its journey, driving my tractor in a smaller and smaller circle, working my way toward the middle of the field and the last narrow swath of standing grass. Had time to mull over Dad too. He reminded me of an old cow we used to have. She was tame as a pet coon one minute, and then, without warning, her cheese would slip off her cracker, and you'd be climbing the closest thing you could find to save your bacon from being trampled. I never ran from Dad, but I wanted to. Who knows what he'd do if I did.

Evening finally came. Deer ventured out—does with fawns at their sides, bucks with nubs of antlers that looked like another pair of ears. One sure-enough dandy buck strutted his stuff across one end of the hayfield. His rack of antlers towered over him, tall and thick, like he'd put his head in a bush and came out with branches stuck to it.

The sun and I finished our work about the same time. I kicked the mower out of gear, drove to the edge of the field, near the road where Dad would pick us up, and parked next to the baler. Cameron finished raking a few minutes later and followed me.

Jake walked to me, his tail wagging him. He put his head under my hand, so I could scratch him, and then moved to make sure I got his back.

I sat down with my back to a tractor tire. Stretching my legs out felt wonderful.

Cameron shut off his tractor, jumped down and walked over. "Dad's late."

"He won't be long," I said. "Wants to make sure we're finished. Might be parked in the woods watching us. You know how he is."

"Don't remind me."

Dad didn't leave us in the field after dark most times. Both tractors had lights, but we had chores to take care of. Chickens needed to be fed, hogs slopped, the garden tended, and dinner dishes washed.

Thoughts of my first wish poked me in the belly with a sharp pang of guilt. After I found out from my friend, Cindy, I could wish on a star, but only if it was the first star in the sky, I wished on a wish. I saw it the next night, put all I had into it, fingers crossed, hoped to die, all the things, and wished Dad would have a wreck. It's not right, I know, but I couldn't help it.

I never considered what we'd do if he crashed his old, blue rust-bucket. Me, Jake, and Cameron could survive without him, that's for sure. Jake could run down rabbits, and coons were right tasty. Some creeks had fish. Nuts and berries could be picked. Hundreds of old barns and houses sat empty in the woods. We could hide out. No one would know. We'd live off the land like folks did in the olden days, before fast food was invented.

My tongue had been dry as a dead rabbit on a dusty road, but now my mouth started to water. I couldn't help that either. Me and Cameron had only been to The Burger Stop once, and Burger Monster…I could only imagine what monster burgers *they* made. People walked into that place fast, like they knew what was cooking. When they left, they barely moved, holding their stomachs, like they were weighted down with food.

Must be nice to eat until you can't stuff down another bite. My belly turned over at the thought.

Cameron sat next to me. Jake plopped down and put his chin on my lap. I stroked his head.

"Cameron, what do you want to be when you grow up?"

"A ninth grader."

"What? Come on. I'm serious."

He laughed. "What's there to be?"

"I don't know. You could be a fireman or a policeman or a farmer."

"Well, I'm not going to be a farmer. I promise you that. I might be a cook so I can eat when I want to. I don't think about such things. All I know is being a kid is killing me, spending our summer vacation from school in the hayfield and slopping hogs. Why would I be a farmer?"

"We don't think alike, do we?"

"Why would we?"

"We're twins."

"Well, maybe if we were identical we would."

Never thought of that one. "I wonder who's the oldest."

"T, we're twins."

"Yeah, but one of us is older. Can't be born at the same time. Just like a hog or a dog."

Cameron picked a blade of grass and held it in his lips like a toothpick. "Does it matter?"

"No, it doesn't."

"I wish you'd stay on a subject longer."

There were too many stars in the sky to be wishing on one. A big one twinkling on the horizon would have been good, but it was never the first to appear. "Do you think there's a God? Look at all them stars. I feel so small, like, like I'm just nothing. Don't you?"

"You are small. So am I."

Cameron always stated the obvious. I didn't know if I wanted an answer, not really. My heart told me God existed. If Jake was an angel, then God was out there somewhere. Didn't angels work for God? "He's supposed to be everywhere at once. Might be sitting right here by us."

Cameron glanced around, as if he might catch God standing on the other side of a tractor tire, listening in on our conversation. "T, you sure got a lot of questions floating around in your head. I don't know about God. Hard to see how He could be everywhere. He sure ain't looked in on us much, not that I can tell." Cameron pulled one blade of grass at a time and made a pile on his pants. "All I know is I'm hungry, thirsty and tired. I've been on that tractor so long I'm still vibrating. Probably be another hour 'fore I'll be able to feel my feet they're so numb."

Now that the tractors were silent the bugs chirped and sang. As dusk's red and yellow shades faded to gray, then to black, the skeeters woke up, their buzz irritating as the no-see-ems tormenting folks during the heat of the day. No-see-ems are always behind you, even when you look back, quick like, they stay behind you, buzzing, driving you crazy. No one's ever seen 'em.

Cameron put a hand on Jake's head and stroked it.

"I'll be glad when Dolly has her calf, so we can start milking again."

"Just another chore for us to do. Don't we got enough without you wishing for more?"

"I suppose, but at least we can get a squirt of milk when Dad isn't looking."

Milk would be good. Milk on cornflakes with a dab of honey would be even better. "Dad said we had to run a trotline on the slough tomorrow." Cameron didn't move. I could tell he was curious by his silence. "I told him he should take you, because you like to fish."

"What'd he say?"

"Nothing."

"That when he slapped you?"

"Yeah, sorry. He knows you like to fish."

"That's why I can't go. Sorry you got slapped."

"He'd a' got me for the tooth on the mower anyway. Just used you as an excuse."

We sat for a minute. We felt comfortable in silence.

I said, "Thanks for saving Jake from the coon today."

Cameron nodded. Before he could reply, Jake's belly rumbled and reminded me. "Did you feed our coon before we left the house this morning?"

"Yep. Give him some water and a couple of eggs."

"Hope Dad don't find out we gave a pet coon his prized eggs. He'd have our hide. Might shoot the coon too."

"How would he know? He doesn't go to the barn except to check on our work. I'll make sure and pick up any shells he left when we get home."

Another rumble coursed through Jake, emerging from between his teeth as a growl. Headlights topped a hill in the distance.

The bugs grew quiet. They knew he was coming too.

Dad drove up and stopped, arm on the window. A tune played on the radio, but there was too much static to hear the words. I lowered the tailgate so Jake could jump in. He gave it a good effort but didn't make it all the way. He held on with his front paws, his hind legs flailing at nothing. I helped him in and closed the gate.

Cameron put one hand on the handle but didn't open the door. He cupped the other hand to Dad's side of his mouth, so Dad couldn't hear him whisper. "Come on, T. Get in."

"You're already there. Quit stalling and get in yourself."

Cameron leaned into me and hissed. "I sat next to him this morning. It's your turn and you know it."

"I don't know nothing of the sort. I had two turns in a row riding in the middle yesterday. This will be your second turn and make us even-steven. If you can't keep the count straight, I'll help you."

Cameron cringed and jerked the door open when Dad's booming voice shook the air. I hopped in.

Dad jerked on the shifter like he did Dolly's teats when he helped with the milking. "I don't know why you let the tailgate down for that old dog. He can jump in or walk. Ought to put him down. Isn't worth nothing."

Talk about killing Jake hurt my heart. He's my dog. Come out of the woods one morning and walked straight to me, wagging his tail. He chose me.

Mouthing off within striking distance of Dad could prove dangerous, but I didn't care. "Dad, that's my dog, and he's good for huntin' coons. I take care of him, and he don't cause no trouble. I'll hurry next time, so you don't have to wait."

Cameron took my right hand and twisted my little finger like a key in a rusty door lock. The lights on the dashboard lit Dad's face just enough for me to see him smile. The smile, one that didn't mean he wanted one in return, and Cameron's pressure on my finger kept the rest of my thoughts from reaching my big mouth.

I glanced at my brother and he turned loose of my hand.

Cameron loved me. I knew he did, even though he never told me.

I'd like to have talked about love with Cindy, and thought I'd found the gumption to do it one day on the playground at school, but my tongue froze up like a stiff drop of tree sap in December, and I broke out in a sweat.

Lights shone from the house. Momma Ray had dinner ready for sure. Probably mashed potatoes and lumpy gravy with fried chicken. She didn't cook much else. Not for me and Cameron anyway.

My mouth watered again.

Dad slammed the pickup in park and turned it off. "You boys get on with your chores. Don't forget to doctor them two sick piglets."

Cameron opened the door and I stepped out. The odor of pig manure soured my thoughts of fried chicken and taters.

Dad walked away, and Cameron whispered, "Ty, I don't want to doctor hogs. I don't give two hoots about them sick piglets."

"Me either, but we don't have a choice. I'll get a stick to hit their momma if she gets after us. I can whack her on the nose and she'll leave us alone. Let me get Jake out of the pickup."

Cameron stood next to me.

Jake went in the dark hole that was our barn without looking back. And him with only one eye to look around! Not me. I wasn't going in there. No telling what might've been in there. Snakes and skunks could've been laid up under the wooden workbench, waiting. All kinds of spider webs crisscrossed the doorframe or hung from the open ceiling. Not to mention the usual residents, like squeaky mice and rats the size of rabbits.

Jake came to the door, then he turned and disappeared into the hole again. It was safe.

Cameron reached in and pulled the string on the bulb hanging just inside.

Jake stared at the little wire cage on the workbench. The coon stared back, standing in the middle of the cage. Coons are smart, and he knew Jake couldn't get to him.

I grabbed a broken shovel handle from an old barrel of garden tools. It fit my hand well. It would keep Dad's sow from taking a bite out of us.

Cameron nodded his approval. "That ought to do it. I got the flashlight, but give me a second."

"Cameron, what are you doing? Let's tend them pigs right quick."

"Just relax a minute. I got a couple of more eggs hid for our coon. Then we'll look at the pigs."

"Just leave it for now."

Cameron ignored me, took two brown eggs from between a pile of dusty tote sacks under the bench and opened the door to the cage a crack. The second he did, that coon came out of there like nothing I'd ever seen. Went straight up Cameron's outstretched arm to the top of his head.

Cameron screamed like one of the girls we chased on the playground at recess. "Help me! T, help me! Get him off!"

Both barn doors stood wide open and the coon could have run out of either one, but he chose to scratch on my brother instead.

Jake joined in the mix and jumped on Cameron, knocking him down. The coon gave up on Cameron's head and left with Jake hot on his trail.

My brother turned on me, like it was my fault. "Why didn't you help me? Now we don't got a coon no more."

"I was laughing too hard to help. That's the funniest thing I've ever seen."

Cameron brushed himself off. He looked kind of huffy, but then he smiled. "I guess I did look a sight. Better call Jake back, if he'll come."

"He'll be back in a minute. He knows we're not hunting. Let's doctor pigs."

Dad liked any kind of hog as long as he could get it cheap. We had red Durocs, black and white Hampshires, and crosses between the two. Breeds didn't mean a thing. If their first name was pig, Dad liked them.

The sow was a Hamp with a black rump, a pink chest and head, and she was huge. She nosed around in the mud at the back of the pen, but stopped and eyed us when we approached, head low, like she dared us to enter.

Cameron shined the light into her coal-black eyes and goose bumps jumped out on my arms. I took a firm grip on the shovel handle, looked at my brother, and crawled over the fence.

4

White clapboard siding gave our house a scaly, menacing look. Brown water stains close to the ground looked like rotten teeth. Windows to each side of a rust-red door were its eyes and nose. Flower-printed bed sheets, Momma Ray's handmade curtains, covered the windows. No lights on, nothing inviting about it, except the thought of a bed.

Curtains didn't make much sense really, not to me. Eyes looking at our house belonged to wild animals and bugs. We lived a mile off the road through the woods, and I don't recall anybody who just stopped in, for whatever reason. People would know they were lost long before they got to our place.

Jake padded along behind us as we walked from the barn.

I couldn't see it yet, but I had my eye on a dinner plate. "My belly's been feeding on my backbone ever since we got home. All I can think of is fried chicken."

"Me too. Might not be chicken though. Whatever it is, it's going to be cold."

"I don't care," I said.

As we neared the door, Jake left us and trotted around the house, out of sight. He had a dark place to sleep in the bushes under the eave beneath our bedroom window.

The swamp cooler stood two-legged at the window beside the door, its head in the window, blowing air into the house. Water trickled down the straw mats. Weeds grew tall under it, where water dripped from the leaky waterline that fed the thing. The noisy fan would cover our entrance, and that was good for us, because the last thing we wanted to do was wake up Dad.

Humidity inside matched the outside, only cooler. I pushed the button on a little light under the plywood cabinets. The pungent odor of propane lingered near the white porcelain stove. Momma Ray had the blackened coffee pot loaded with water and grounds, ready for morning. I replaced the lid on the container she kept near a burner, so the pilot light would keep the bacon grease in it warm.

Can't cook without bacon grease.

On the table sat two empty glasses, two plastic plates with a scoop of mashed potatoes, and one greasy chicken leg. The glasses were a ticket to all the well water we could drink.

Cameron's shoulders slumped when he saw what she'd put out. He picked up his plate, inspected it for a minute, and stuck a finger in the taters. He slid back the wooden bench we normally used and sat.

I filled our glasses and took a chair facing him. We couldn't change what she'd set out, and griping about it didn't make sense, so I picked up my fork.

Cameron acted like he didn't want his, but the first nibble of cold potatoes opened the floodgate, and he ate with a fork in one hand and the chicken leg in the other. He gnawed on the leg bone until the only thing left to do was crunch it up and swallow it, like Jake would.

He sat up, wiped his hands on his pants, and looked at my plate. I didn't eat as fast and had a couple of bites left. He licked his lips and let out a long breath. He could just keep on licking. I was hungry enough to lick the grease off of my plate.

As the last bite entered my mouth, he stood up and walked to the icebox.

"You know they don't keep nothing in there. All the food is locked up in the icebox in their room," I said. Like he didn't already know.

Cameron opened the door and extra light from the bulb inside flooded the kitchen. He slammed it closed and stared at the opposite wall, toward Dad's room.

A look of hate or disgust, it didn't matter. I knew how he felt.

Cameron let out a long breath and pointed a thumb over his shoulder. "Only got a yellow box in there."

"It's been in there a long time. What's it for anyway?"

"Baking soda. Momma Ray says it absorbs odors. Got to have food in there to make odors."

"We ought to put it outside. Maybe them hogs would smell better."

Jake whined at the screen door. Always the gentleman, not one to complain or be pushy, but he'd sat patient long enough.

I pushed away from the table and checked the slop bucket. Two T-bones lay atop of some stuff that it would take my biology teacher to identify. I picked them out and gave them the once-over.

Cameron stepped forward for a look. "Any meat left on them?"

I shook my head and heard a sigh.

Jake took them as a gentleman would, then turned and trotted off behind the house. He'd lie in his bed and gnaw off enough to let him sleep. Maybe he'd stay home tonight and not go gallivanting through the woods looking for a rabbit or a squirrel to eat.

The sink only held two glasses and some silverware and didn't take long to wash up.

I turned to Cameron. "You done? Give me your glass."

"Yeah, I'm about real done."

"What's that mean?"

"You'll see."

He handed me his glass and stomped across the kitchen louder than I would have liked.

"Cameron, I don't want to see. I want to know."

He disappeared around the corner into the dark living room.

After checking the kitchen, I turned off the light and tiptoed down the hall, closing the door separating our room from the rest of the house as I went. The swamp cooler blew it open, so I secured it with a folded piece of cardboard wedged between the door and the jamb.

I crawled into bed next to Cameron. He liked to take up more than his half of both the bed and the covers, especially in the winter. Tonight it wouldn't matter much, because it felt like a steam cooker in the room.

We'd been sharing a bed since forever, so we didn't know of another way. Neither of us had ever wet the bed. That made it easier.

Most boys wouldn't think of sharing a bed with another boy, at least not a single bed, not even with a brother, but we didn't mind. In the winter, it was the only way we could stay warm, since Dad demanded the hall door be closed at all times.

A slight breeze drifted across the room between two open windows, cooling the sweat on my legs and chest. The sheet stuck to me like flypaper.

Crickets and other bugs sang their night songs. Jake chewed on a bone below the window. Dim shadows on the wall grew darker and more distinct as the moon peeked over the treetops.

"Thanks for helping with the hogs, T."

"I thought you were asleep."

"Nah, just thinking about things."

"What kind of things?"

"Want to sneak out?"

Holy cow, my heart just stopped beating right then. I rolled over and propped myself up on an elbow.

Cameron laid there, his back to me, acting like the question was normal or something.

"No, I don't want to sneak out. You done lost your mind."

"I might want to sneak out. You wouldn't tell, would you?"

"Course not. Just quit talking about it." I laid back.

"I might quit talking, but I'm not going to quit thinking."

I tried to block his question from my mind by concentrating on shadows swaying on the wall. "What would you do? Where would you go?"

"You said to quit talking about it."

"Cameron, come on."

He turned onto his back and put his hands behind his head, like me. "So, did Dad say what time you were going fishing?"

He was trying to change the subject. "It's a long ways to the road. Take awhile to get anywhere from here."

"I don't care. I just want to do something I'm not supposed to. That would give me one up on Dad."

"We just did chores. We could have stayed outside, would have been the same thing."

"Nah, we were supposed to be doing chores. Crawling out the window is different. Answer my question."

"He just said the missus wanted some catfish."

Cameron blew a puff out his nose. The bed shook with the effort. "The missus? He talks to us like we're not part of the family. I wonder what he has planned for me?"

"He didn't say."

Cameron turned his back to me again. His foot touched my shin. I think he felt better when he touched me. Knowing he was there made me feel good.

I watched shadows change shape and listened to the night, afraid to go to sleep, in case he tried to sneak away without me. Life without Cameron would be … well, this morning was the first time I'd ever thought about losing my brother. I didn't like the feeling.

My eyes burned and grew heavy. Too heavy.

A sting on my cheek, a mosquito, and then one buzzed my ear. I jerked the covers over my head and turned onto my side.

Alarms went off in my mind. Asleep. Are you crazy? Skeeters in the house?

The screen was missing from the window, and Cameron was gone.

5

It was all I could do to keep my mouth closed. I wanted to scream out the window. No Cameron and no Jake, now what? My best friends had run off together.

The first hint of morning glowed orange through the oaks behind the barn. Our old rooster would be screaming his fool head off any minute.

Leaning out the window, I grabbed the screen propped against the house and put it in place. At least Cameron put it where I could get at it. Probably by accident. While I tried to think of a story, any story, I shoved my feet into a pair of socks, buttoned my shirt and jerked on my britches.

What could I tell Dad and Momma Ray that they would believe? Nothing, that's what, nothing at all. I headed for the kitchen.

Voices floating down the hallway made me wish to die. I stopped in the living room to listen.

"Honey, how's your coffee?" Momma Ray cooed.

"It's just right, dear. It's always good when you make it."

Oh, I almost gagged.

Momma Ray said something too low for me to hear. Sounded like air leaking again. I stepped closer to the door, where I could just see the back part of the stove.

Smooching noises mixed with the simmering gurgle of coffee on the burner.

Chills ran up my spine and goose bumps jumped out all over me. That kissy-smoochy stuff didn't set well this early in the morning.

Dad's deep voice sounded too close for comfort. "I'm going to take a boy down to the river with me today. Going to run a trotline and catch some fish for us."

"Well, that sounds wonderful. Who you taking?"

"Ty."

Silverware clinked in the sink. Water splashed. A noisy sip and sigh followed by a cup scraping on a plate put me on my toes. I edged a little closer.

Momma Ray cleared her throat with a dainty *ahem*. "Can I use Cameron around the house while you're gone? I got some things he can do for me."

"Why you sure can, Ma. Better use him good today. Don't waste no time. I got me a little deal working with a man in town. He's going to pay me to work the boys a day or two. Speaking of, I better get them up."

Dad's comment about working us for someone else didn't register right off. When it did take root, I didn't have time to mull it over. A chair slid across the floor.

I stepped around the corner, rubbing my eyes, like I'd just rolled out of bed. As I entered the kitchen, Cameron strolled through the screen door holding a handful of eggs.

Dad looked back and forth between us. A look of recognition changed to confusion then to doubt. He focused on Cameron, the one out of place. "Boy, what are you doing outside this early?"

Cameron walked by him and placed the eggs on the counter. "I couldn't sleep. Thought I'd gather eggs and start our chores."

Momma Ray looked like she didn't believe the story either. But what could they say? There he stood with a double-handful of eggs.

Dad looked at me and started to say something, but he must have changed his mind. Apparently, he knew something had happened, but he couldn't put a finger on it.

He stood and handed his coffee cup to Momma Ray. "You two sit down. Momma, fix them an egg apiece." He pointed at each of us in turn, wagging his finger. "You two eat and get your chores done. Ty, me and you are going to the river. Cameron, you're going to help here at the house today."

Cameron let out a hard breath. Dad paused and gave him a narrow, glaring eye. Cameron managed half a smile, and Dad looked away.

Momma Ray's lips turned down at the corners. She crossed her arms over her nightdress, curtains with different flowers. It was too short too. Cameron called them very-close veins. She had a bunch of them on her legs.

She never said anything to support us. This morning was no different. I think Dad scared her as much as he did me and Cameron.

Dad walked out and she turned her attention to me, pointing with a spatula. "Your shirt's crooked."

Redoing my shirt and watching her to make sure she didn't catch me, I leaned over and whispered to Cameron. "We get outside and I'm going to poke you in the nose."

Cameron never moved anything but his lips and whispered back. "You do and I won't share the eggs I found and hid in the woods."

That revelation changed everything. Sometimes Dad and Momma Ray left us with the chores and went to town. We could sneak in and have our own little feast if that happened in the next day or two. Eggs hid outside wouldn't last any longer than that. Coons would find them.

Momma Ray put a blob of grease in the pan. Me and Cameron sat silent, listening to the eggs sizzle and pop. They were hard and crispy-brown around the edges when she slid them out of the skillet onto our plates.

I ate and kicked Cameron under the table.

He kicked back.

Cameron looked at his egg like he did the chicken leg and taters. Then it disappeared in two bites.

I cut mine up, ate little pieces at a time, and took my time chewing.

Cameron stared at every bite, but I didn't care one hoot.

Jake walked up and took a peek through the screen door. Yeah, me and Jake were going to have us a one-on-one about him running off with Cameron. It's not that I didn't appreciate him looking after my brother, but he should have barked or whined, anything to let me know what was happening.

The floor groaned as Momma Ray shuffled back and forth across the kitchen in her purple slippers. Time and moisture had weakened nails, curling floorboards at the joints in a few places. The gray paint had worn thin in front of the sink and the stove, revealing dark knots in the oak.

Cameron looked at Momma Ray for the first time as she dropped the spatula in the sink and walked out. "T, quit kicking me."

"You run off and left me. You and Jake." My voice broke, surprising me as it squeaked out.

"I didn't leave you. Just went out and looked around. I felt free."

"If a skeeter hadn't bit me on the cheek, Dad would'a found you gone. He might have killed me. I don't mind taking a licking for you, but friends shouldn't leave like that. And why didn't you put the screen back on?"

"Too tall, I tried. I didn't think about the skeeters eating on you."

"No, you didn't think about nothing." Something had a hold of my heart and wouldn't turn loose. My words sounded strange to me, like someone else gave them to me to say.

Cameron looked like he recognized me for the first time. His hand rose slowly. I took it and we shook. My tears tasted salty.

A door slammed in the back room. I wiped my eyes real quick. Momma Ray walked in carrying a slab of baloney and a loaf of white bread. Me and Cameron looked at each other then eyed the meat. Nothing like a good slab of boloney fried to a golden brown to make a feller rub his tummy.

As Momma Ray worked at the counter, it was obvious what she did was not for our tastes. Dad and I were going fishing. Dad would want a hefty lunch. She cut a good slice and set the knife aside. "You boys know school starts Wednesday."

You could have pushed me over with a broom. Summer was done already? And the information, for our benefit, simply stated. Cameron blinked like he'd got caught downwind of Dolly after she passed gas.

I grinned and thought of Cindy's red lips and

freckles, and colored barrettes holding her golden hair behind perfect ears. And green eyes and a sweet smell, like rain in the morning. She made me stutter.

6

Jake fell in beside me on the way to the barn. He raised his dark head to cast a lazy eye at me every other step. I knew what he wanted—a morning hug and a scruff on the head. One side of me wanted to hug him. The other side wanted to ignore him for leaving me asleep and running off into the night.

Jake nosed the slop bucket. "Quit, Jake. I'll get you something out of it before I give it to the hogs. I didn't forget your breakfast. I should leave you on your own, but I'm not like you and Cameron. I think about my friends."

Cameron trotted up beside me. "Want to see them eggs?"

Fire stoked in my belly. "No, I don't want to look at no eggs."

"I got eleven of them for us. They're in the fork of that crooked oak behind the barn."

I wanted to see them and gave the oak a peek. It would be something to hide from Dad if I knew exactly where they were. "Cameron, we can't sneak into the house and cook, so why look at them? One egg for breakfast this morning just made me hungrier. The sight would make it worse."

"I just thought you'd want to see them, that's all. You still mad at me?"

Cameron didn't get it. I stopped and put my hands on my hips. "I have to spend the rest of the day in the boat with Dad. I'd rather cut hay."

"Yeah, well, I thought I'd ask. Tell you what. You watch the sow while I check them piglets, and I'll help you get stuff ready to go fishing."

I didn't answer right off, but I thought *why not?* Doctoring pigs alone would make me nervous with that big sow watching every move and smacking her lips like she had peanut butter stuck to the roof of her mouth. "That's not what Dad said to do, but sounds good to me."

I held the broken shovel handle while Cameron looked at the piglets. When finished, we checked the fishing gear.

Cameron walked around the boat and inspected it. "This boat's embarrassing. It's not as long as the pickup. Not as wide neither. Got a kitchen chair mounted on the bench in the front. Looks like hillbillies own it. Aluminum, probably made out of old soda cans, and that old motor, can't even read what it is anymore."

"They do."

"They do what?"

"Own it. The hillbillies."

We laughed.

I mucked wet, moldy leaves out of the bottom of the boat. "Dad likes to sit in the chair and act like a captain, perched up there in the front, giving orders, swiveling around and pointing. Keeps him out of my hair. Let's go find the lifejackets."

Jake followed us to the barn and back.

Cameron put in the lifejackets, two foam blocks with straps holding them together.

Dad would whack me if I forgot the minnow bucket. I made sure to grab it. The trotline was rolled up around a stick with the rusted hooks stuck in each end and tucked under the bench seat in the back, by the motor. The wooden oar, in case the motor quit, lay hidden in deep grass under the trailer. I freed it and stuck it under the seats.

Cameron raked leaves out with his fingers. "I wish Jake would sit and quit following us everywhere."

"He's not following us."

"Yes, he is. Everywhere we go. To the barn and back, to the back of the boat, to the front of the boat, around the boat. He tags along everywhere we go. Then he sits and watches us."

"He's following me, watching me. He's my dog. You just happen to be with me."

Cameron nodded. "He does take to you. I'll give you that. I better see to the rest of our chores. I didn't finish this morning."

I kneeled to mess with Jake. The next thing I knew, I was on all fours. Jake growled and pushed, trying to get his head under me. He rolled onto his back and put his paws against my chest. His skin was so loose, like a badger, he could about turn over in it. I straddled him. His ears lay flat on the ground, lips loose, teeth showing, and eyes big. Like bat-dog. I loved him. He got the hug he wanted earlier.

"Hey, boy. Get up."

Jake pushed me off, flipped over, and scurried under the boat.

I stood and brushed at my pants. Dad carried a black lunch box and had a silver thermos tucked under his arm.

"I got everything ready, Dad. Just need to hook it up."

"You get the cool box?"

My face must have given me away.

"Boy, get the cool box, and tell Cameron to come here."

Jake led me to the barn this time. He glanced back toward Dad and the boat once or twice. I grabbed the red and white plastic ice chest and yelled for Cameron.

Jake stayed in the barn when we left, watching from the doorway.

Dad turned around his pickup and hooked the boat to the bumper. The cool box fit in the bow.

"Cameron, you get chores done and get to the house and help your ma. Watch your lip. I'll be home later. You remember that."

Cameron looked like he'd taken a big swig of sour milk and I knew why. Momma Ray was not our ma. We were young, fourteen, going into the ninth grade, and we knew how moms were supposed to be. We had one, a real one, just hadn't seen her in a while.

I crawled into the pickup before Dad had to tell me to.

Once we left, I forgot about things, or at least the conflicts that ruled my thoughts. Dad wasn't a talker, so the countryside led my mind.

Lots of houses much nicer than ours were tucked back off the road. Big stone barns with painted doors, some of them displaying the owner's name or a brand in large, white letters, overlooked beautiful green pastures and fat cattle. Next to those fancy places were trailer houses with gray, wooden stairs, green or brown shutters and trim. In their yards stood a swing set, a blue plastic swimming pool, or an old car on blocks, half hidden by deep grass and weeds. Sometimes all three.

One car had the hood off and turned upside down

next to it. Three kids stood in it. One boy held a stick over his head. He might have been the captain of a pirate ship, or fighting wild Indians with his brother and sister.

Me and Cameron fought Indians before we came to live with Dad.

Cows and horses of every color stood in belly-deep grass. One horse looked up as we passed and got me to wishing I could ride one someday. Kids at school talked about going on trail rides and roping and barrel racing and stuff.

It seemed like everyone owned a tractor, a nice big one with an air-conditioned cab mounted on it. Some kid was lucky.

Fall wasn't too far away if school was about to start. Leaves would change color, and that was good because the weather would cool and skeeters and no-see-ems would leave folks alone.

The thought of school brought me to the holes in my britches and loose soles on my shoes. My knees stuck out of my pants and they were a good four inches too short. Momma Ray had ironed a patch on both knees, but her work didn't last a week. Maybe patches would last longer on another kid, but not on me. Cameron had grown so much his britches looked dumb. Almost didn't cover the top of his socks.

Dad pulled in at the bait shop. "Boy, you throw in the minnow bucket?"

"Yes, sir. It's in the boat."

Dad didn't shut doors. He slammed them. He disappeared inside with the yellow bucket.

I figured he'd buy goldfish or minnows. Large minnows would be better. Goldfish had sharp fins on their backs.

When Dad walked out with the bucket, the cheek-lady followed him. That's what me and Cameron called her because she grabbed our cheeks and pinched the fire out of them. Dad looked like he'd swallowed a dose of stink bait and hurried to get away.

She dogged his every step. "You know you need to. Don't ignore me, Mr. Ray. Last time I seen your boys they were skinny as a rail. You start feeding them. Looks like you get plenty to eat."

Dad shuffled to the boat and never said a word.

Then, she spotted me. "Well, which one are you? Ty? Oh, you darling! Let me look at you!"

Dad looked relieved when she turned her attention toward me.

I panicked. She had her hands raised, warming up her pincers, and here she came.

Jerking the door open, she grabbed me by the arm and pulled me out of the pickup with a surprising grip. She smelled like I don't know what. Coffee and cigarettes mixed with stump water and peppermint.

She started squeezing and thumping me like a watermelon. "He's thinner now than he was a month ago. You ought to be ashamed, locked up. He looks like he's got worms."

She quit poking, pushed me back inside the cab, slammed the door, and scurried around the front of the pickup to meet Dad at his door. I couldn't believe her boldness. She walked right up to him and put her finger in his face, and she was a good foot shorter too. "Mr. Ray, the next time I see them boys, they better have some meat on their bones. Don't you look away, and don't look down your nose at me. You think I'm afraid, you got another thing coming. I'll tell you something else. Get them boys in church. Let them meet the Lord. Just because you don't want to know Him don't mean they don't."

She held Dad still with a finger. His eyes moved as the red fingernail did—up, down, left, and right. When it shook, he blinked.

Then I heard something I had never heard before. Dad whispered, "Yes, ma'am."

The cheek-lady marched back toward the bait store, her pant legs slapping together, elbows working at her sides. She stopped at the door, looked back, and swiped at a strand of brown hair blowing across her face. "Ty, darling, you be a good boy." She waved and disappeared inside.

Dad crawled in behind the wheel and slammed the door.

I thought I'd missed something. His lips had moved and "Yes ma'am" had emerged. I heard it, but before we got on the highway, not fifty feet from where we were parked, I convinced myself there was no way. He never said it.

I pretended to check the boat, turning to look through the back glass. It dawned on me when I saw Dad's jaw muscles flexing, I might be in a heap of trouble.

The cheek-lady meant well, but I wished she had minded her own business.

7

The Duck River is lined with trees. Hickories, red oaks, maples, and walnut trees stand tall on solid ground, and when the leaves turn, they are a beautiful sight to see.

That's where Dad nearly flipped us the first time we put the boat in the water, so we didn't go there anymore. Both Dad and the motor on one end at the same time pointed the bow at the sky. That day, he was going to drive because I sure didn't know anything about driving a boat. He cranked her up, put her in gear, and gave it too much gas all at once. Nearly drove the backend under the frontend. Scared the daylights out of me. I fell into the back of the boat, piled at Dad's feet.

After that, I drove the boat. Dad was my teacher and the lesson wasn't much fun, but I learned how, and now, Dad sat and pointed while I drove.

Dad turned left and right down dirt roads choked with brush to the slough. I knew where we were going but still got confused. The grass was deeper, the bushes thicker and taller. The muddy road ended at the edge of the water and that's where he backed up the boat to put it in.

A swarm of skeeters greeted me as the door opened. Jake would have checked for snakes in the deep grass and weeds. He would have made me feel better if he could have came.

We undid ropes holding the boat and let it slide off the trailer. Dad gave me his lunch box and thermos to put in.

"You should have said something!" Dad yelled. The lid on his feelings didn't stay on long.

Say something? That was a first. My thoughts went back to the cheek-lady and how she had given Dad what for. That made me want to run for the woods, but my feet were sucked down in mud and wouldn't move.

"Look what you made me do." He pointed to the back of the boat. "The plugs ain't in."

I managed to back up a step as he stomped to the front of the trailer, grabbed the winch rope and hooked it to the ring on the bow of the boat. "Here, get over here and crank on it, boy."

We let the water drain, installed the plugs, and started over.

Once the boat settled in the water and we had all of our gear in, I crawled to the back and let the motor down. Dad said it had fifteen horses, but it didn't run like fifteen of anything, and it sounded like one of Dolly's calves with a bad cough.

Dad used his cap to brush off his captain's chair and plopped down. The boat rocked and bobbed, adjusting to the sudden shift in weight.

"Pull out the choke before you start pulling on the rope. No, squeeze the bulb on the gas line and pump it up first. It's been awhile since we run it."

It had been a while, all right—a year. Used it and parked it. Probably wouldn't start in ten years without some work.

I started pulling and knew right off we weren't going anywhere.

"Did you pull that choke out like I told you?"

I checked it to make sure and pulled the starter rope some more.

"Open the throttle halfway. Don't stop. Keep pulling. Wait, I smell gas. Boy, you got it flooded. I ought to kick your behind."

Since I did what he told me, how did I flood it?

We cautiously traded places and Dad got loud and colorful. That's how he worked on things. The less he knew, the louder he got, and the redder his face turned.

Pretty soon the bottom of the boat held pieces of motor. I ran back and forth between the boat and the pickup, getting wrenches of this size and that size out of the toolbox. In between runs, I tried to watch where the parts came from on the motor. But in the end, who knew? I hoped Dad did.

Then, it dawned on me to wish otherwise. We could go home if he took it apart and couldn't put it back together. This might be our last trip. I had a good feeling about it too.

Dad stopped removing and started replacing. He'd blow on pieces before he put them back. When he turned a part over and looked at it a second, he'd grow still. His lips pooched out and face wrinkled. Then, looking down his nose through the bifocals of his black-framed glasses, he'd work his lips, pucker, spit over the side, and put it on.

It started. I couldn't believe it. Second pull and it sputtered to life. He gave a satisfied grunt and we traded places again.

I backed us into the slough. Dad turned his captain's chair to face forward and waved us on. The throttle stuck at first, but I managed to point us down the middle between overhanging trees and bushes without an incident.

She tracked dead center, but Dad made adjustments as he saw fit. He pointed left and right, and I just sat there. He leaned when he pointed and his arms were heavy, so the boat rolled to the side he pointed to and naturally went in that direction. Soon as he pulled his arm in, we'd go straight.

Dad's ears were sunburned and red. Peeled patches looked sore. Below his hairline, a dark mole seemed to grow bigger as I stared at it. A bead of sweat snuck out from under his gray ball cap, found a wrinkle, and followed it toward his shoulder.

We stopped to put out our first set of hooks between two low hanging tree branches about twenty paces apart. Dad tied the knot in the trotline on the first branch, then used the oar to pull us along to the next one.

I put a big minnow on each hook and never poked myself, not once. At the second tree limb, Dad stretched the line tight and tied another knot.

Dad rowed and spit a lot. Now and then he poured a cup of coffee into the thermos lid and sipped at it. Something nasty always sat in my throat when thinking about that combination.

It took three pulls before the motor fired. When it did, I put it in gear, opened the throttle to the little rabbit stamped on the handle, and turned hard right to move us away from the bank.

Dad reached for what wasn't there. His coffee cup flew over the side of the boat, his legs pointed skyward, and he did a flip off the chair and landed in a heap in the bottom of the boat. It only took a split second, but it seemed like several minutes. Dad cussed a blue streak, screamed, "I can't swim," then let out another round of words I had never heard before.

As he rolled to his knees, I managed to cut the power and look up. Lights flashed, then went out.

I felt like I floated on a cloud. My feet hit something soft and mushy. Cold crept in on me, as if Cameron had all the covers and wouldn't share. Surface and air were above me, but just beyond my fingertips. It was like looking through the bottom of a glass, light shining through murky water, shadows extending through the water to bottom. I took a breath and my lungs filled with water.

Pushing with my legs, I surfaced and grabbed a branch, choking and gasping for air. How come I'm in the water? And where was this water? Nothing seemed real. Splashing noises behind me caused me to turn.

Dad had the paddle out, rowing my direction. The look on his face showed determination, but to what intent I could only guess.

My mind came back, and I knew I wasn't going to take a chance. I pulled myself hand over hand through the bushes toward the bank until my feet found bottom, then I waded ashore.

"Come here, boy. Get back in the boat. I didn't mean to push you out."

My tongue found a loose front tooth and my upper lip felt like a marble attached to my face. My blood mixed in the water dripping off my chin and turned the front of my gray T-shirt red.

Dad tapped the oar on the edge of the boat. "You hear me? Get back in here."

What he expected was beyond me. "I'm not swimming back out there. You want me in the boat, you got to come here." The words came out strong and defiant, surprising both of us. Dad seemed to relax and let the oar rest on the edge of the boat.

Snakes lived along the slough, lots of them, but I didn't care. The danger lay in front of me.

Dad's tone changed to something I'd never heard before, not when he talked to me. "I sure didn't mean to do that. Come on, Ty. Get in the boat. We'll go home."

He sounded sorry, but not for one minute did I believe he hadn't meant to hit me in the face. In fact, I had an idea. He gave it to me when he screamed like a girl and said he couldn't swim.

8

Cameron stood and tossed a large weed out of the flowerbed when we drove into the yard. He pushed up his cap and passed the back of his hand across his beet-red forehead. As Dad and I stepped out of the pickup, he started toward us but stopped. I didn't catch Dad's look, but it made Cameron bend over and pull weeds again.

Jake ambled over to walk me to the back door. He put his nose against my wet pants and sniffed up and down, first one leg then the other. A pat on his head was all I could muster before going inside.

From the living room, I noticed Dad pass a window, then another.

Momma Ray worked in the garden dressed in red pants and one of Dad's green long-sleeved shirts. A big straw hat covered her head. With her yellow rubber gloves, she looked like she should be standing on the highway next to orange cones holding a sign that read *Slow*.

I moved to the window where I could hear them but remain out of sight.

She stood and clapped the mud from her hands. "You're back early."

"Yeah, the boy fell out of the boat and liked to drowned on me."

"That's terrible. Is he OK?" She looked around like I should have been following Dad.

Huh, she sounded concerned.

"Oh, he's fine. Just got to whining about being cold. We only got out one set of hooks, but I'll take him back with me in the morning. We should have some nice fish on by then."

I'd just tell the same story Dad just told if Momma Ray asked me questions. She'd have to ask too. I wouldn't volunteer information about what happened.

I had to go back to the river with Dad. Perfect.

In the bathroom mirror, I inspected and wiggled the loose tooth with a finger. Boy, I'd look dumb if it fell out. I sure wasn't going to pull it, and neither would anyone else. Not if I had anything to do with it. Unless it died and turned black, then it would have to go. Missing would be better than black.

I peeled off my shirt in the bathroom, washed out the blood in the sink, then changed clothes and hung my wet ones on a string in front of our bedroom window. It took several rags stuffed in my tennis shoes to soak up the water, at least enough to stop them from squeaking when I walked.

After a minute, I gathered the nerve to go outside. Had to face him again sooner or later. Cameron motioned to me with a quick wave, looking over his shoulder at the same time. I walked over and crouched in the flowerbed.

"T, what happened? What happened to your lip?"

"Dad hit me in the mouth."

"What'd you say?"

"I didn't say a word. He wasn't in his chair good and I dumped him out of it. Gave the boat motor too much gas."

Cameron looked like he'd just swallowed a stinkbug.

I continued. "It's like he fell ten minutes before he hit bottom, grabbing for air the whole time and nothing there for him to hang on to. You should'a seen it."

Cameron's eyes brightened. "Wow, I wish I could have. I would've laughed."

"No, you don't wish nothing of the sort, because I shut off the motor and woke up on the bottom of the slough. I don't even remember looking at Dad. Must have sucked in a gallon of swamp water. Probably swallowed a tadpole too, for all I know."

Cameron bared his teeth, like Jake warning me Dad was coming.

I pulled up my lip. "Look at my tooth. It falls out and I'll look like Billy Ardmore. Bet he hasn't got five teeth in his head. Has to gum his food in school, and that stuff's just mush at best."

"How'd you get out of the water? You can't swim much better than me."

"I don't know, but I did. That's all that counts. I'll tell you something else. Remember the cheek-lady down at the bait shop?"

Cameron put his hands on his cheeks. He didn't have to answer.

"She give Dad what for when we stopped to get minnows. Really laid into him because we don't have meat on our bones. Told Dad we might have worms."

Cameron's shoulders hunched. "Worms? How do you have worms? We don't eat worms. That's just dumb."

I shrugged. "I'm just repeating what she said. And she told Dad to take us to church too."

"No she didn't."

"Yes she did. Just like that. She poked at him with

her finger."

Cameron kept talking, asking questions about the cheek-lady and what Dad said and did. It made me feel better. I didn't want to tell him what I really thought. I knew he'd go along with it, but I didn't know how to tell him. He'd have to lie for me if my plan worked and lie if it didn't. There was too much to remember when lies were told. We needed to have a meeting, off in the woods somewhere, where no one could walk up on us. Or better yet, maybe he didn't need to know anything. Then he wouldn't have to lie.

Cameron chewed on the information about the cheek-lady just like I had. No one had ever talked to Dad like the cheek-lady had. At least not that we'd ever witnessed.

"T, what's today? Sunday, I think."

"It's Sunday. There were cars at the white church, and I seen them folks down the road in that big stone house walk out in their go-to-meeting clothes and get in the car. Why, what are you thinking?"

He looked toward the back of the house. "You think Dad would let us go to church today?"

My tooth smarted when I forgot and rubbed my tongue across it. "He's not thinking about taking us to church. He ran back there to Momma Ray and started telling about what happened. Made sure he got in his story first. Said I fell out and liked to drowned on him. Bunch of baloney."

"You don't know what he said."

"Yes, I do. I heard him through the window when I went in the house to change clothes."

"Good thing you got to listen in."

I couldn't help what came out next. "Cameron, do you really want to be free?"

9

When Dad walked around the corner of the house, Cameron and I had our heads down, weeding the strawberries. He looked like he couldn't believe what he saw and was lost for words. Probably thought the right jab he'd delivered to my face had straightened me out for good. Made me the perfect son.

Jake had found a wet, shady spot and scratched out a hole to lie in. Just another hot, lazy day for him to sleep through.

Dad watched us a minute and walked away. The screen door slammed. Me and Cameron glanced at each other because we knew he was going inside to take a nap.

I rocked back to sit on my heels. "Here it is. When I cranked the motor over hard and Dad fell, he screamed that he couldn't swim."

Cameron squinted, his forehead wrinkled and lips pooched out.

I was going to have to spell it out. "Cameron," I held my hands up. "I'm going to…"

I heard something behind me and turned as Jake padded up and sat next to me, ears pricked my direction. Heat rose in my face and guilt flooded my soul like nothing I'd ever felt, even after telling a lie. Jake was my angel, my watcher, and now he was trying to listen in on my conversation.

Cameron waved his hand in my face. "Hey, wake

up. What are you going to do?"

Jake never moved. He didn't want me to scratch his head or pet him. Just waited for me to open my mouth. I couldn't. Not now. "Jake, go lay down. Go on."

I waved my hand at him, but he never raised a paw, only moved his head as my hand passed by. "Jake, get! Go on!"

Cameron shook my arm. "T, you're yelling. Dad's going to hear you."

I threw a weed. My temper flared toward my friend, and I yelled, "Quit staring at me, you one-eyed monster!"

Jake's ears dropped and he trotted toward his hole, eyeing me over his shoulder.

I'd convinced him to leave, so we could talk in private. Then, my heart sank because of what I'd called him. I'd insulted one of my best friends.

The screen door banged, and I knew I was wrong on both counts. Cameron had tried to warn me about yelling, and Jake knew he was coming.

Cameron threw a muddy clod at me. With a broken voice, he said, "I told you. Why don't you listen?"

Dad stormed around the corner, shirtless and barefoot. He'd already turned red. His rage brought Momma Ray from the garden to watch. Hands with yellow gloves at her sides, she stood in the flowerbed. A haggard scarecrow with rosy cheeks dressed in a baggy shirt and a straw hat. Emotionless.

Poor Cameron. Because I didn't listen and wouldn't keep my mouth shut, Dad vented most of his anger on him first. I'd get my turn, but it wouldn't last as long and wouldn't be as violent. I guess if Dad had a favorite, it was me. He saved me for last. The best for last? I don't know.

When Dad finished with Cameron and started on me, Jake howled from somewhere in the woods close to the house.

I kept my head down. My tooth meant more than the rest of me. I could hide bruises with a shirt and pants, or make up an excuse. I knew how to make good excuses. Fell off the tractor, slipped with a wrench, ran into something in the dark, or had a pig get after me. But I didn't want to gum my food or be afraid to smile.

Dad ate well, grew fat over the years, and didn't work hard, so he didn't last as long. He gave us one last kick in the behind and sent us to the barn to start our chores.

Enough pain over enough time will dry tears. I'd made up my mind to never cry again. Cameron too.

Behind the barn sat several drums, tall weeds in and around a stack of bald tires, and a broken-down push mower. Dad's attempt at a chicken house stood naked, its frame leaning to one side. Next to it, a pile of gray boards full of rusty nails and an old yellow washing machine.

I hopped onto one side of the washing machine, Cameron onto the other, our backs together. Jake plopped down at my feet and laid his head down, stretched out on his paws.

My tooth was something I couldn't keep my tongue off of. Like meat stuck between two molars only a toothpick could dislodge.

I shouldered Cameron. "I'm sorry. Kind of lost my head."

Cameron let his foot bang on the side of the

washer over and over. "You better leave that tooth alone. It might set again if you do."

"How did you know I'm messing with it?"

"Been watching you."

Two chickens pecked their way around the corner of the barn, both white but one speckled with black like it roosted under Dad's pickup and got oil dripped all over its feathers. Like our pigs, Dad didn't have a breed of chicken, just colors, all colors. White, red, black, and one blue Bantam that laid green eggs. The rooster was a flogger. He was dark red and black with a large red comb on his head, sharp spurs on his legs, and mean enough to use them if you got too close.

"Cameron, do you remember loving Dad? I know that's not something we talk about, but didn't you love him at one time?"

"How come you asked that?"

"I don't know. I loved Dad. Couldn't wait to meet him when Mom told us about him. Remember our surprise when she said we had a dad? We used to talk about him all the time."

"That's because we were young and dumb." Cameron laughed without humor.

A hawk passed overhead as the thoughts in my head fluttered in and out. "I don't know if I love him now though. I think it's turned to hate." I mulled over that feeling a second. "I wonder what Mom's doing?"

Cameron stopped kicking the washer for a beat then continued. "What time is it?"

"I don't know, seven o'clock or about."

"She's drunk."

"Yeah, I figure she is too."

Cameron whispered, "If she changed, quit drinking and running around with those men she used to bring home, maybe she'd come get us."

I laughed this time. "No, people don't change, brother. Dad hasn't changed. Momma Ray hasn't changed."

"You never told me what you planned before you started yelling at Jake."

I eased off the washer. Guilt came back and sat heavy on my chest. *It's now or never, watcher angel or no watcher angel.* "You said you felt free the other night, when you snuck out, remember? Well, I think I have a way for us to be free forever."

"How's that?" Cameron turned and looked me in the eyes. Then he hopped down.

"Dad can't swim. I think I'm going see how he likes it on the bottom of that slough tomorrow."

10

Cameron edged up to the corner of the barn. "I don't see him."

I peeked over his shoulder. "Nah, he isn't coming out. Too tired after whupping on us for interrupting his nap. Had to take a longer one."

"Momma Ray ain't even looked our way. Just pulls weeds. Don't bother me none, except I managed to sneak and eat a couple of tomatoes without her seeing me earlier. I wouldn't mind doing that again if she'd disappear inside the house."

"You didn't save me one?"

Cameron stood up straight and moved his hands up and down his body as if to say, "Look, dummy, where am I going to hide a tomato?"

The point made, I pulled at his shirt. "Come on. The sun's getting low. She'll go inside and cook supper for Dad soon. They'll be in there like two lovey-dovey birds, cooing back and forth, watching television."

"Yeah, and eating. That's something we won't be doing, not for a while away."

Clouds rolled in from the north bringing darkness and skeeters, both earlier than normal.

Jake hadn't paid much attention to me since I blabbed my plans. Cameron could ignore me, often did, but Jake never ignored me. He looked away when I glanced at him, like I'd disappointed him or hurt his feelings and he couldn't stand the sight of me.

Jake's an angel for sure.

My gut gnawed and twisted at my insides and not from hunger. Guilt wasn't an unfamiliar feeling. It just hadn't lasted as long before, or made me so uncomfortable.

We snuck into the house a few minutes after the last light went out in Dad's bedroom. Two pieces of bread with honey smeared on them awaited us. The bread must have come from the bottom of the bag, the dregs of the loaf. It was on the verge of falling apart in our hands and wouldn't go down without water. The honey tasted wonderful.

I checked the slop bucket for something Jake could eat. Not much there, but I poured it out in a tinfoil container for him anyway. He sniffed at it then looked into the night like he had another option. I closed the door and left him to it.

In bed, I put my hands behind my head and stared into the dark. The big oak outside the window couldn't muster a shadow on our wall, not with the clouds hiding the moon.

"What you going to tell the cops?"

Cameron's voice gave me a start. The question surprised me. "What do you mean?"

"Just exactly what do you think is going to happen when you dump Dad out of the boat? The police are going to ask you a million questions."

The police? My stomach flipped.

Cameron stirred, shaking the bed, his voice a whisper. "I been thinking about it. You tell them Dad fell out. You gave it too much gas, turned the motor, and ker-plunk. You tried to help him, but he's so fat you couldn't. That's what you tell them. Nothing else. You got to cry too. They'll want to see you cry, or they won't believe your story."

"What if he floats? What'll I do then?"

"Heck I don't know, T. Run over him with the boat."

Kill Dad? It hit me. Cameron and I were talking about murder, planning a murder, and it was my idea. This didn't begin in my mind as murder. Oh, why did I open my big mouth?

"Hey, are you listening to me?" Cameron shook me.

"Yeah, I'm listening."

Cameron talked and I listened, but I didn't hear. Could I really do what I said I would and set us free? After committing murder, even if I got away with it, how could I be free trapped in my own guilt? After sitting with the feeling for a couple of hours, I didn't know that I *could* live with it.

He either grew tired of talking or realized I wasn't going to answer and turned his back to me. After a minute, his breathing leveled out and he slept.

Time passed and gray replaced black. If I slept, I didn't know it. Time was running out.

The next thing I knew we were doing chores again. Chores were never ending. Chickens, pigs, garden, and when a calf hit the ground, milking twice a day. Our hay would be dry soon, so we'd be rolling bales after school.

Jake stayed in my shadow, but I didn't pay him any mind. He didn't bug me to pet him or wrestle. I'd look at him and he'd blink and look away.

The sun hung in gray clouds like the heart in my hollow chest. My mind was in turmoil. My world was about to end, and I felt helpless to stop it.

Dad strode from the house as me and Cameron

looked over our fishing supplies. To our surprise, he bent over the bumper, unhooked the boat, and let the trailer tongue fall to the ground with a bang.

My heart beat again.

The door slammed. Momma Ray walked from the house, black purse hanging from the crook of her elbow, swinging at the pace of her short, stuttered walk.

Dad stood and took a deep breath. "You boys get in the house and have your breakfast. We got a chore in town to take care of. When you get done, get busy pulling weeds in the garden. We won't be long." He pointed at me. "You and I are going back to the river when I get back."

Dad and Momma Ray drove off as we walked up the concrete steps. Cameron opened the screen door and stopped. He cocked his head, listened, and then turned toward me. "Let's get them eggs."

Holy cow, my heart soared. I forgot all about them. We were going to eat this morning. Didn't need a good front tooth for eggs. We ran for the oak tree.

~*~

As he cooked, Cameron blew what I'm sure he thought sounded like a tune. He couldn't whistle and sounded more like a leaky tire. He only managed to emit a squeak every other puff.

I took a peek at the frying pan. "Did you use plenty of grease?"

He gave me a sideways glance. "Well, course I did. I found a slice of bacon in the slop bucket. I'll heat it up and we'll split it."

Oh yeah. Getting better all the time.

Jake sat at the door. He knew what we were doing, and he knew he'd get a share of it.

I kept an eye on Jake. He'd be our first warning when Dad returned.

"Cameron, don't forget we got to hide the eggshells in the woods."

"I know. I put them in the slop bucket. We'll dump it in the hog pen when we get through. They'll disappear in there."

Cameron liked his eggs hard. Jake and I didn't care, though the white had to be cooked before I'd eat them. Jake would lap at them all runny if he had to.

With the two eggs Momma Ray made, we had a total of thirteen. Cameron divided them evenly, right down to cutting the last one in two, six and one-half a piece. He put our plates on the table. I poured water for us, then let Jake in and slid two eggs off my plate into the foil container for him. Cameron started to eat, then stood and gave Jake an egg.

We ate with deliberate motions. Even Jake seemed aware of the special moment and picked at his portion. Cameron cut one bite, placed the knife next to his plate, picked up the fork, ate a piece and chewed.

When he finished, Cameron pulled a thin stick from his shirt pocket, put it between his teeth, leaned back in his chair and clasped his hands over his belly. "Boy, what luck. Couldn't have been better, I'm telling you."

Cameron was right again. "Doesn't get no better." We reached across the table to slap hands. "How's your face and neck?" I asked. "Did Dad say anything to you?"

"About what?" Cameron put a hand to his neck.

"That coon scratched you up. They hurt?"

"Nah, I don't feel anything."

The screen door bumped against the jamb. I jerked, and my heart jumped in my throat. Jake had nosed it open and walked out. He glanced back on the way down the steps with a look that seemed to say, "What? He's not coming yet."

We laughed as the tension eased.

I stood with my plate. "Come on. Let's put everything back where it belongs before they come home and catch us."

"I don't care if they do. This was worth a good licking."

We cleaned and inspected the area to make sure nothing would give us away. I grabbed the slop bucket and opened the screen.

Cameron stopped me. "Well?"

"Well what?"

"You goin' to do it?"

11

Dad seemed different when he got back from town. He carried himself different, dejected or beaten down, even cowed. I couldn't put a finger on it and thought maybe it was just me, but I saw Cameron looking at him funny. Something was up.

Momma Ray got out of the pickup and marched toward the house with her nose in the air, elbows working at her sides, purse swinging in one hand, papers clutched in the other.

I couldn't imagine what might have happened. They could've had a fight, but Dad led those. He didn't lead this. Momma Ray didn't have papers in her hand when they left, so that might be what made her grouchy.

Dad hooked the boat up. "Ty, get in the pickup. Cameron, you get back to the garden. We won't be long. Just going to check the trotline. When we get back, you boys got a job in town to do for Mr. Jordan."

I forgot. I meant to tell Cameron that Dad planned to make money off of us.

Cameron started to say something, looked at me and took a step in my direction.

Dad pointed toward the garden. "Cameron, you don't need to talk to him. Go on and do what I told you."

Cameron watched and when Dad turned, he held his hands behind his back and gave me a thumbs-up with one and crossed fingers with the other.

Guilt returned.

I didn't want to think about Dad on our ride to the slough, so I put my mind to pondering Mr. Jordan. He was the mayor or a councilman, something big like that. I'd seen him a couple of times and he always had on a fancy coat and tie and polished cowboy boots. His kid, Randy, was a few years older and kind of uppity. He talked to me and Cameron like we worked for him. Now it looked like we were going to. Good thing he moved up to high school last year or he'd rub our noses in it in front of the whole school.

What kind of work could we do for a rich man that he couldn't hire out good and proper? Must have a ton of money hidden somewhere, a big house and a fancy car. Big city guys had to make a lot of money.

Clouds threatened rain. We didn't need it, not with hay down. Much more than a sprinkle and we'd have to turn it so it would dry. That meant more work. It would get me out of the boat and Cameron out of the garden. Too much rain would turn it all black and rotten. Only a cow can eat rotten, moldy hay. I don't take much to ciphering in school, but I know moldy hay doesn't sell for much.

To my surprise, Dad turned in at the bait shop. The cheek-lady warned him that I better have meat on my bones the next time she saw me. That was yesterday and I didn't feel different. Dad risked another tongue-lashing.

When Dad got out of the pickup, I followed him. I wanted to hear it if she had at him again.

A man with a small net leaned over a big silver tank full of water and minnows. He looked up. "Can I help you?"

Dad didn't look at him. He turned down a row of nets, stink bait, lures and the like. "Two dozen big minnows and two large bags of ice will do."

The man nodded and propped the net against the tank. "Did you bring your minnow bucket?"

I didn't wait for Dad to look at me. The lady wasn't there so I wouldn't miss much. I ran out to the boat to fetch it and brought it to the man.

"Thanks, son. What's your name?" He stuck out his hand. "I'm Weldon."

"I'm Ty." I took the hand. It was cold and damp from the minnow water. One crooked finger stayed straight. I squeezed.

"Son, look at me."

He kept my hand and squeezed it harder, but not too hard. His eyes were deep blue, intense, the kind that could see into me. He grinned, his teeth crooked but white, the sweet smell of fruity gum on his breath.

"When you shake another man's hand, look him in the eyes."

"Yes, sir." I squeezed back hard as I could, eye to eye.

He turned my hand loose and patted me on the shoulder. "Hand me that net, Ty. I'll put some minnows in your bucket."

"Yes, sir."

Dad walked up. "Boy, take the ice to the boat and put it in the cool box."

"Yes, sir." I picked up the plastic bags and walked out.

Dad brought the minnow bucket out a minute later and got in. "What'd he say to you?"

"Nothing, just asked my name."

Dad spit out of the window and put the pickup in

gear.

I didn't look at him. He didn't look at me. His jaw could have been flexing, but the chaw of tobacco stuffed in his cheek made it hard to tell for sure. Dad was hard to read. He could explode at any time. Even with a smile on his face.

We worked in silence, untying the boat. I put in both plugs, tightened them, and helped push it off the trailer. Choke, but not too much choke, and it started right up.

Dad mounted his perch. He'd been quieter than I'd ever seen him. Not that he said much at all to anyone on a good day, but something stuck in his craw had him by the tongue.

The sun had yet to show its face. The day was easy on the eyes, no glare off the water, and cool, a hint of fall in a slight northerly breeze.

I eyed my father as we motored to the set of hooks. Cameron's words echoed in my ears, his thumbs-up and crossed fingers etched in my mind. I hadn't answered his question. *Could I? Much less, would I?*

Could I say I hated my father? Yes. But I didn't want to hate him. I tried to remember, but couldn't recall he'd ever said he loved me. Not even "good job" after a hard day's work.

Dad leaned over, opened the cooler, took a piece of ice, and let the lid fall. The slough was plenty deep. We were in the middle. Just turn hard left and Cameron and I would be free of him. I rubbed my tooth and sore lip with my tongue, looking for a reason.

I steered straight.

Dad centered his mass in the chair. He propped his feet on the bow and leaned back.

My chance passed.

The red mole on his neck looked bigger, full as a tick, ready to pop. The backs of his arms were white to the elbow, rosy pink to the wrists, with sunburned patches. His blue shirt bulged at the seams.

A Red-Tailed hawk soared over the treetops. A small blackbird chased him from behind, moving in on swift wings. The cheek-lady dogging Dad came to mind. As the hawk cleared the last branches over the slough, it flipped over and struck out with its sharp talons, but missed catching the blackbird and fell from the sky like a rock. My stomach fell with it. At the last second, just before crashing into the water, its wings unfolded and it soared again, gaining altitude. Its shrill screech echoed through the trees over the drone of the motor. Before it disappeared in the distance, the blackbird resumed its attack.

Dad watched every move the birds made, shook his head, and whistled low and soft, like *wow what a sight*.

The warmth of a blanket on a frosty night came over me, and I knew I couldn't harm my father.

I wanted to yell for joy. Something down deep, a feeling I'd never felt before, wrung my heart until my eyes ran with tears.

12

I'd never felt the kind of tears that flowed down my cheeks, nor could I describe the feeling that came with them. Optimism or hope? But in what or for what? My soul had received good news, but it didn't register as something I could put into words.

All the bad of the last nine years—Mom giving us away one day, waking up in hell with Dad the next— ran from the corners of my eyes, down my cheeks, dripped off my chin, and pooled at my feet in the bottom of a dirty boat. Dad could have turned to look at me at any second, and I wouldn't have had an excuse, nothing to say for my blubbering. But he didn't. The flood ran its course. The clouds cleared. The sun shined on a new me, a new feeling.

Crying didn't go with the good things in my life. I didn't know tears of joy. This cry ended too soon.

The boat slowed to a crawl as the notch on the throttle passed the little turtle stamped on the handle. Our trotline lay around the corner.

A red-breasted hummingbird darted by and disappeared into the trees. A minute later, it returned with a smaller, green-breasted mate, dipping and diving. They sang their own song, a happy tune, like a kid walking up the street with a plastic whistle. They were small and quick, hard to see, but the tune gave them up wherever they traveled.

Water roiled in a dozen places between the two

large branches we'd tied the trotline to. Big fish made a ruckus like that, or a lot of small fish. Someone passing by, unaware of the line of hooks, would sure wonder why the branches shook the way they did.

Now, if they were catfish and not carp, we'd have something.

Dad swiveled around and reached for the oar. "Shut the motor off, boy."

"OK, Daddy." I pulled the red button. The wake chasing us lifted the backend then the frontend as it passed and raced toward shore.

The boat drifted in close with the help of Dad's rowing. I took the line, pulled in the first catfish and grabbed him behind the head, careful of his sharp, poisonous fins, and removed the hook from the corner of his mouth. A poke with a fin will make the area sore as the devil for a day or two. The fish might have weighed three pounds.

Dad took him from me, put him on the stringer tied to the boat, and dropped him over the side into the water.

Big minnows were easier to catch than little ones, but they were still slippery. After chasing them around the minnow bucket with my hand, I finally grabbed one and put it on. Dad pulled us along with the oar.

The next fish didn't weigh anything, a slight tug at the most. I pulled once, twice, then, the fish pulled so hard both of my arms went into the water to the elbows.

"Watch out boy. Hang on to him. That's a real fish we got there."

Dad leaned to help me, but only made things worse. "Daddy, be careful, we're taking on water!" I turned loose.

"What did you call me? Where did that come from?" Dad sat back and grabbed onto both sides of the boat.

"I'm sorry, Daddy, I just thought…"

"Don't call me that. Since when do you call me 'Daddy'? That's three times you said it." He regained his seat and motioned at the water where the fish went under. "What'd you turn loose of him for? You had him. He'll get tired after a bit and give up. Just hang on. He gets off I'm going to boot you in the rear. Get a hold of him."

Where "Daddy" came from was a mystery. It just came out. "I won't let go again. You think there's room in the boat for him?"

A dark blue tail bigger than my hand broke the water's surface.

"There's room. You hang on this time. Soon as he quits fighting, stand up and pull him in."

"Yes, sir."

The big cat jerked me around long enough for Dad to get involved again. "Pull on him. Not like that. Hold the line up. Boy, you'd better get after it. Get mean with him."

Before the fish tuckered enough for me to stand, my arms ached like I'd been bucking hay bales all day, and my hands were turning numb from the thin trotline wrapped tight around them.

It's a wonder I got him in the boat. Every time he'd about clear the edge, Dad thought he needed to lean over to help. Like to have dumped me out twice.

"Boy, that's got to be the biggest cat I ever seen come out of these here waters. No telling what he weighs. Thirty pounds I bet. You won't believe the filets I'll get off of him."

No, Dad, I'll believe it. What I won't believe is if me and Cameron will get to eat one.

Dad hoisted the fish and turned him slow like, looking him up and down, a big smile on his face. He'd be telling someone about his huge catch down at the coffee shop tomorrow morning. Me and Cameron were going to have to hustle out and find some more eggs to hide tonight, just in case he left to brag and took Momma Ray with him.

He pulled the stringer up, put his prize on it, and then gently lowered him over the side. He looked at me. "What? What are you looking at? Quit your gawking. We won't put on no more minnows. That fish there will be plenty. We'll run the rest of the hooks, taking fish off, then roll the line up and take it home. I'm going to tell you something else too. Don't ever call me 'Daddy' again."

13

White, boneless filets came off in slabs. Dad looked like Jake drooling over a bone, even whistled a tune. I'd heard it on the radio, but couldn't remember the words—something about crying and dying and pickup trucks.

Dad skinned fish and cut meat until the cooler stood half-full. It took both of us to slide it in the back of the pickup between wads of orange baling twine, a flat spare tire and a shovel.

He opened the lid, gave another satisfied grunt, let it fall and slammed the tailgate. "Come on, get in the pickup. I told old man Jordan I'd have you boys to the house by two, and it's pushing that right now."

"Dad, what kind of work are we going to do for him?"

Dad cocked his head and wrinkled his nose, so his bifocals moved up and made his eyes bigger. "That's a dumb question. You're going to work. What difference does it make what kind of work it is?" He opened the door and climbed in. The pickup started, then died. He had to crank on it a few seconds again before it coughed and started. "The only thing you need to do is work. Don't ask no dumb questions, and work. And don't you mess up like you do in the hayfield neither. You better not get fired 'cause you don't watch what you're doing, you or Cameron, either one."

If I thought Dad would fire me for messing up, I'd

do it more often. I didn't mess up on purpose. It just happened.

Cameron looked like he was about sweated down when we pulled in the yard—rosy wet cheeks, shirt soaked through. He stood, arms at his side, shoulders slumped.

Dad got out and unhooked the boat. "Cameron, don't just stand there like you got no sense. Get over here." He pointed to the cooler. "You two take that in the house and get back out here. Hurry up."

Jake dragged himself out of the shade in the barn, so I could give him a scruff on the head.

We grabbed a handle each. Jake padded back to his lair.

"Cameron, we caught a fish that must have weighed thirty pounds. Or that's what Dad said."

Every stride I took, the cooler hit me in the leg. I tried to adjust my step to match Cameron's, but it got worse. "Quit bumping the cooler. That hurts."

"You didn't do it."

I'd been thinking on that. Murder was done all the time, but people never got away with it. Always opened their mouths and gave themselves up.

"Obvious, ain't it? I couldn't do it. You sound disappointed."

"I am. Makes me want to cry. Why couldn't you? Didn't get a chance or what?"

"I had plenty of chances. Something told me not to."

Cameron pushed hard on the cooler, but I was ready for him and pushed back. He talked through clenched teeth. "You believe a dog is an angel and now you're hearing voices. I didn't tell you not to. I've been hoping to see the cops drive up all day. Now I know why they didn't. Aren't you tired of your heart jumping in your throat all the time? It's not supposed to beat up there. I'm just plain tired too."

We placed the cooler on the kitchen table. Momma Ray would bag up the fish and put them in the freezer in their bedroom to make sure we couldn't put our hands on any.

"Cameron, I just felt like something's going to happen. Someday soon, we'll get out of here. I know it."

"Someday? You know how long that is? It's just like 'maybe'. That's all we've ever heard. 'We'll see', 'someday', 'if you're good.' Ain't one of them arrived yet." Cameron leaned in close and jabbed an elbow into my ribs. "Too bad *you* didn't drown yesterday."

Tears rose to overflowing and streamed down my cheeks. "What's that mean? You want me to die?"

"No, don't be dumb."

"What then?"

"You'd be free of all of this. Even hell would be better."

"Don't talk like that. Hell wouldn't be better. Folks are on fire down there."

Cameron grabbed my elbow. "We almost went down there, and you know it."

"I don't know nothing of the sort."

"If we'd killed each other, we would have gone there. Both of us for murdering the other one."

"We were kids, we're still kids, and dumb ones too. Like you mentioned before. Just look what we've become." I pulled my elbow away.

Cameron laughed.

I thought he'd really gone off to the duck farm then.

"T, we tried to choke each other to death. That's real dumb. Think about it."

I had to agree, but laughing? It wasn't a laughing matter. "Cameron, look at these filets." I opened the cooler. It was time to talk about something else.

His eyes grew wide and he blew a good puff that had a hint of the whistle on Momma Ray's old teapot. "Boy, that's some fish all right. Come on. Let's go before Dad blows up. Maybe Mr. Jordan wants us to weed his garden, and we can eat some of his tomatoes."

14

Cameron grabbed the door handle on the pickup and pulled it open. Then he stood there expecting me to hop in. "No way, Cameron. Your turn." I pointed a thumb to indicate which way he needed to move, in case he didn't get it.

A cheek rose enough to close one eye and pull his mouth out of shape. His head and shoulders sagged. He was mulling his options. It was his turn and he knew it. I followed him in and pulled the door closed.

Dad didn't talk, at least not to us. We didn't have conversations. Unless he had a task for us to do or we'd made a mistake, he never said a word.

Cameron kept glancing at him. Like he had something he wanted to say. I hoped he'd just be quiet. Silence meant a lot around Dad. But no, Cameron piped up. "Dad, what kind of work are we going to do?"

Dad had his right arm propped on the steering wheel. He looked over his glasses at me. "Ty, tell him."

The words spilled out of my mouth quicker than my thoughts. "Work and don't mess up like we do in the hayfield and get fired."

Cameron looked at me sideways, without turning his head, and mouthed, "What?" like he didn't believe what he'd just heard. His jaw worked. All he needed was a chaw of tobacco and a window to spit out of. I let him chew on it without seasoning the thought with my input. Dad might whack him if he didn't be quiet.

Farms, woods, and grasslands gave way to blocks of houses as we entered Ozark. Downtown, the streets radiated from a central square. Most of the businesses shared a common wall, and large, plate-glass windows provided an eye into each store. The occasional awning, sign, or red and white striped barber's pole hung from brick storefronts to give a hint as to the products and services sold inside.

A doughnut shop sat on one corner. I'd gone there a couple of times, but long ago. It was probably where Dad met Mr. Jordan, since the city's center was just down the street. Most likely, Dad would sit at the bar there, drink coffee, and brag about the biggest catfish he ever saw.

We turned onto a narrow, paved road shaded by huge oaks. A large barn with brown stone across the bottom came into view. Above the big double doors stood the letters "AJ" painted in white. As we neared, I could see a matching stone house with lots of trees and bushes around it. Looked like several peach trees in the bunch. Peaches would be good. It was that time of year.

To live on a place so big, in such a nice house, would be something for sure. Maybe someday.

Dad slowed, then turned between two huge logs planted in the ground holding another log across their top. It must have been thirty feet tall and as wide, with a forest of red roses growing to each side. Someone mowed the grass beside the road.

Unbelievable. The "J" on the barn stood for Jordan, and we were going to work here.

"You boys sit. I'll see if the old man's around." Dad opened the door, pulled the chaw from his mouth and tossed it into the bed of the pickup. He looked around, worked his cheeks, spit, and wiped his forehead with the back of his hand.

A tall, thin man with a slight limp strode from the barn. He pulled off his straw hat and waved Dad over. He looked confident and sure, even nice. "Don, come in here a minute. Bring your boys with you."

Dad motioned for us to get out, and then he slammed the door.

Beautiful wooden stalls lined the alleyway through the barn. Each door split in the middle, upper and lower. The bottom sections were closed. Hooks on the wall beside each door held nice leather halters.

Two big red horses looked at us. One stretched out his head toward me and took a sniff as I passed.

The tall man in the straw hat stood at an open door toward the middle of the barn. Thumping sounds came from inside. A man in short chaps and a cowboy hat walked out with a horseshoe, put it on an anvil, and gave it a couple of raps with a hammer. His chaps had narrow pockets for his hoof knife, clippers, and rasp.

"Don, how are you?" The tall man stuck out his hand and Dad shook it.

"I'm real fine, Mr. Jordan. Sorry, I'm a few minutes late."

Boy, Dad sounded like he was gushing. He didn't dare call him "old man" to his face.

Mr. Jordan looked at me and Cameron. "Well, introduce your boys."

He took a step toward me.

Dad pointed. "That's Ty. The other one's Cameron."

Mr. Jordan stuck out his hand.

I grabbed it and looked him straight in the eyes. "I'm Ty, Mr. Jordan. Nice to meet you."

He shook hard, real hard. His blue eyes sparkled.

Cameron stuck out his hand and shook but didn't look him in the eyes.

Mr. Jordan bent a little at the waist to look into Cameron's face, and then turned his hand loose.

Dad grabbed Cameron's elbow and shook it. "Look at the man when he's talking to you, boy."

Mr. Jordan eyed Dad, then waved him off. "That's all right, Don."

Two Red Heeler dogs moseyed over to give me a good sniffing. I gave them a scruff that started their stubby tails to wagging.

Mr. Jordan bent and patted one. "This is Buddy and Jake. They just come over to be sociable."

"I have a dog named Jake," I said.

"You do?"

"Yes, sir, but he's just a one-eyed coon dog." I glanced at Dad to make sure he wasn't giving me the shut-up eye. "He, he lost it one night chasing a coon."

"Well, I bet he's a good dog. Don, I'll have them home about seven, eight at the latest. Hope that's OK? I know school starts the day after tomorrow."

"I'll come get them. No use in driving out to the house."

"No, sir. I have a meeting downtown this evening. It'll work out just right. When we get done, I'll bring them home."

Dad lowered his voice. "Well, then, if you insist. That'll be fine."

The discomfort in Dad's face was easy to read. He looked like he might need to go into the house and sit for a spell.

As Dad walked out, Mr. Jordan took me and Cameron by the shoulders. "Come into the house a minute. You boys remember my son, Randy? I think he's a couple years older than you are."

"Yes, sir, I remember him." I walked faster to keep pace with his lanky stride. I liked the man. His gray hair and easy manner made me feel comfortable and welcome.

"Well, Randy's been sick. I know he'll want to see you."

I didn't have a good opinion of Randy, but what could I say to his father? Cameron had a sour look on his face. The thought of Randy had spoiled his give-a-hoot.

Dad drove away, his eyes glued to the rearview mirror.

Mr. Jordan led us to the back door, a big, sliding glass thing encased in stone. A cool, sweet, mouthwatering aroma rushed into the afternoon heat as it slid open.

The kitchen was almost bigger than our house. Its black-tiled floor glistened like water, reflecting the island stove and copper pots hanging from the rack above it. To one side, a dark wooden table with a dozen matching chairs stood on a large red and blue rug. Above it hung huge deer antlers with small lights scattered through them. Pictures and paintings of horses hung on the walls.

"Ma, this is Ty and Cameron Ray. They're going to help me awhile today. Maybe this weekend too."

Mrs. Jordan pulled a potholder off her hand and walked around the stove. A wisp of gray hair swung across her forehead. A dusting of flour covered the bananas printed on her apron.

"Hi, boys. Can I get you something to drink? I just made some chocolate chip cookies too." She waited a heartbeat for us to answer then baited the offer. "They'd go good with a glass of cold milk." She opened what I thought was a cabinet, but it turned out to be the icebox with oak on the doors.

Cookies sounded like the best idea I'd ever heard. Me and Cameron exchanged looks.

Mr. Jordan answered for us. "Set them up, Ma. They look like they could use a cookie before we start. You boys sit here." He motioned to one end of the large table and pulled out two chairs. "Come on, don't be bashful. I'll be right back." He put his hat on the knob on the back of a chair.

The cookies were big as an egg cracked in a pan, hot and full of chocolate chips. She gave us two apiece, with a large glass of milk. They tasted like a dose of heaven.

Cameron inhaled his, but not me. I savored every gooey bite. The chocolate tasted bitter, but sweet too. Just right. I didn't notice my sore tooth.

Mrs. Jordan worked around the kitchen with a smile on her face. When our milk hit bottom, she refilled the glasses. I felt like giving her a hug and asking her if I could help her do something.

"Hey, boys. Remember Randy?" Mr. Jordan pushed in a wheelchair.

Randy was bald as a newborn piglet.

15

Randy managed a weak smile. He lifted his hand for a short wave then let it drop onto his lap. "Hi, Cameron, Ty."

Mr. Jordan pushed the wheelchair to the table.

I was shocked. Here sat someone who used to make fun of me. My heart ached for him now, all the sharp barbs he'd uttered forgotten. What do you say?

Cameron licked chocolate from a finger. "Dang, Randy, what happened to you?"

I wished Cameron would've kept his finger in his mouth and bit down real hard. My shoe against his shin under the table got me a hard look.

Mr. Jordan pulled out a chair and sat. "It's all right, Ty. He didn't mean anything. Just doesn't understand, do you? Well, neither do we, but we know the Lord will work it out." He patted Randy on the hand. "Son, you feel up to a cookie? Mom just got them out of the oven."

Mrs. Jordan walked over, kissed Randy on the head, and then fussed with the front of her apron, waiting for a reply. Her green eyes never left Randy's face.

Randy took a deep breath, but he didn't speak, as though it took too much effort to make the words. He shook his head.

I couldn't find words either. He didn't look so menacing and uppity—not now. He was all boney fingers and sunken cheeks, all of him pale. And where did his hair go?

Mr. Jordan smiled and stood. "Well, son, that's enough for one day. Ty, you and Cameron want to wait for me by that white Chevy out there? I'll be right out."

I managed to find my tongue. "Randy, I hope you get better. If I'd known you were sick, I would have brought you a present or something."

Like a rock striking a rock, a quick spark flashed in his dark eyes then went out. His voice was faint, but clear. "Thanks for the thought, but that's OK. Bye."

I didn't know how I turned my back and walked to the door.

Cameron slid the big glass closed and followed me across the yard. "That was dumb. Told him you'd a brought a present. What was that supposed to mean?"

"Presents are nice to get when you're sick. And I would have—had I known."

"How would you know about getting presents? You never got one."

"I didn't know what to say. You didn't say nothing."

"Exactly. Nothing is sometimes best. You think I talk too much."

"What's the matter with him, Cameron?"

"I don't know, but they had to cut all his hair off 'cause of it. I hope it ain't worms. He's awful skinny."

That comment gave me a shiver.

Mr. Jordan walked from the house. He stepped high, his smile bright as before. It didn't make sense to be so happy when your kid was sick and looked like Randy did.

"Come on, boys. Hop in and let's run down to the

lower forty. You know how to buck bales, don't you?"

"Yes, sir," I told him.

Cameron looked like the milk soured in his belly and had risen to sit on the back of his tongue.

Dad was right. Work was work.

The lower forty, as he called it, had two thousand bales on it if it had one. A pickup pulling a long flatbed trailer with four guys following and picking and two guys stacking, worked the far side of the pasture.

Mr. Jordan backed up to another trailer, a smaller one. "Boys, open that sack on the floor there. I got you each a pair of gloves. We're going to load a few bales on this trailer and take them to a friend of mine on the other side of town."

Me and Cameron jumped out, slipped on our gloves, and started toting bales. Mr. Jordan hooked up the trailer.

A small Jeep pulled up, and the man who'd been putting shoes on the horse got out. His shoeing chaps covered his bowed legs down to the knees. He rolled the sleeves of his blue shirt down and buttoned them.

Mr. Jordan glanced at him. "Ed, you drive and we'll load."

"Yes, sir, Judge." He adjusted his tan, sweat-stained hat and gave me a wink.

Man! A judge, not just a city guy. This man put bad folks in jail.

Mr. Jordan continued. "Ty, you jump on the trailer and stack. Cameron and I will toss them to you. Run them across the trailer to start. This won't take long, and we'll go to town."

Thirty minutes later, we had one hundred and twenty bales on. Me and Cameron switched out once, just for fun.

We sat on the hay and shared a jug of water as Ed drove us back to where we started.

Mr. Jordan shook hands with Ed. "Mind if I ride to the house with you? We need to talk about that red mare. Ty, can you drive?"

I didn't know what to say. "Well, I can. I can drive our old boat. We drive tractors, but I've never driven a pickup before."

Ed grinned and winked at me again. He produced a red bandana from his hip pocket, pulled his hat off and wiped it out, then folded the red cloth nice and neat and put it back in his pocket.

Mr. Jordan looked, I don't know, like he was thinking on an important subject. He started to say something, then paused and looked at Ed. "I'll see you at the barn in say," he checked his watch, "thirty minutes. You mind hanging around until we can talk?"

"No, sir, take your time. I got a few things I can do. See you, boys." Ed gave us a quick salute.

Mr. Jordan pointed at his pickup. "Cameron, you jump in the back or get on the trailer and sit down. Ty, you get in the front, no, the driver's side. As soon as you learn how to drive, you and Cameron can trade places, and I'll teach him."

Well, Cameron could have blown me over with that big weenie puff of a whistle he blows all the time. We were going to learn how to drive. I was nervous as a cat sneaking food from a dog's dish.

"Ty, relax. A clutch is a clutch, pickup or tractor. Put her in first and just ease it out, slow like, and give it a little gas. We'll go a ways, then try shifting gears."

"Yes, sir, Mr. Jordan."

"Don't forget you got a trailer of hay back there, and Cameron is sitting on it. You don't want to buck him off."

"Yes, sir."

Me and Cameron had no trouble. We drove all over the pasture. I'm sure the other men picking bales thought we'd fell off the rocker. Mr. Jordan even let Cameron drive us up to the barn, and he did great. He looked like he stood a foot taller when he got out and stretched. "Proud" was written all over his face.

Mr. Jordan clapped as he walked around the front of his pickup. "Good job, men. You're ranch hands now. Relax here a minute. I need to visit with Ed before we go."

When he walked out of hearing range, Cameron elbowed me. "What kind of job is this, eh? Cookies and milk, load one measly little old trailer with hay, and learn how to drive. This ain't right. Dad must owe him a bunch of money or something. I'm telling you."

"Oh, quit your whining. Maybe this is how it's supposed to be when you work for someone."

"Ty, he's a judge. He don't need no hillbilly kids working for him. You see that barn and house? Look at this place. You think he had Dad bring us here so we could see his sick kid and learn how to drive?"

"Randy looks terrible, like he's going to die. That has to be sad for his mom and dad, and sad for him too."

"Yeah, I suppose. I'll say one thing. Mr. Jordan never missed a lick. Picked up half of them bales himself. He talked the whole time too. The weather this and the weather that and something about the hundredweight on the price of cattle, like I'd know something about that. He asked about Dad, Mom, Momma Ray and school. He wondered why we didn't play sports. Why would he care about all of that stuff?"

"Cameron, Dad would have driven, forced us to run to keep up, then yelled about how long it took. Might'a got a good licking today too—just because."

Cameron looked toward the barn and ran a gloved finger across his nose. "I tell you one thing. I ain't telling Dad we learned how to drive and ate cookies. He won't let us come back."

16

I had a million questions on the tip of my tongue, but didn't know how to utter the first word. Cameron sat with his hands on his lap, content to look out the window. He seemed less trusting of our job today and he wouldn't say why. But then that was Cameron. He had to see something for himself before he'd believe it. He could be slow to forgive and forget too.

Dad's old truck didn't have an air conditioner, unless you counted driving fast with the windows down. It didn't have a lot of things. This one was sure fancy. Automatic windows and door locks, cold air blowing and all kinds of gadgets and dials displayed on the dashboard. And it rode real smooth and sure smelled good. Jake might even have trouble hearing this one coming up the road.

Mr. Jordan turned the fan up a gear and held his hand in front of the middle vent. "Y'all getting plenty of air? I appreciate you men coming to the house to help me today. Randy usually helps, but since he's been sick, well, I just like to have some young men around."

Cameron sat up straighter and opened up. "Did the doctors shave all the hair off of him?"

Mr. Jordan laughed. "No, the medicine he took did that. He's been on chemotherapy, and it causes your hair to fall out. It'll grow back now that he's off of it."

"Is he going to be OK?" I asked. "He looks real

sick."

"Ty, well, sir, I…" He downshifted and turned on the right blinker.

A narrow, well-kept lane led to a house with clapboard siding, not unlike our own, but the grass was mowed short and neat. It looked much nicer than ours. The small, red barn behind the house didn't have a brand painted on it. Attached to one side was a chicken-wire cage with the odd white feather stuck in the wire.

"Boys, no one knows why things happen to one person and not another, or why bad things happen to people, good folks and the bad folks alike. We have to have faith. The Lord is in charge, and He loves us and has our best interest in mind."

"What's faith?" Cameron asked my question.

Mr. Jordan stopped in the middle of the lane and put the pickup in neutral. "Faith is hope in something, for something, you can't see." He looked at us. "You understand that? No, well, how do I say it? I have faith, hope, that God exists even though I can't see Him. I have faith that Heaven exists, and when I die, I'm going there to live for eternity. And I have faith my son will get well, grow to be an old man and have many children, like you boys. Faith that God is in charge is the only reason a man can keep a smile on his face and step light when his son is sick."

I could see I might have faith, believe in something I couldn't see, but Cameron? I didn't know if Cameron could.

Mr. Jordan put the truck in gear and pulled around the house to the barn.

A short, thin, black-headed lady, wearing jeans with a shiny belt and buckle, red top, and white tennis shoes, walked from the house. "Hi, Judge. I didn't expect you today."

"No, Elizabeth, I hadn't planned on coming, but I managed to find two good hands to help me this afternoon. This is Ty and Cameron Ray. To tell the truth, I hoped to surprise you and have this load in the barn for you when you got home from work. We're running a little late."

Her white teeth flashed and she extended a slim, firm hand for us to shake. "I'm so glad to meet you. I'm Elizabeth Daniels. You can call me Liz. Let me get the doors, Judge. The hay goes in this end, shouldn't take us long."

We helped her with the doors, propping them open with a brick each. The inside of the barn had a slab of concrete on one side, where a few bales were stacked against the wall. The other side had half a dozen stalls made out of green tube-steel. A brown and white paint horse stood looking at us.

"So, boys," she turned and grabbed a broom and scoop shovel to move them out of the way, "school starts Wednesday. You're going to be in the what, eighth grade?"

Cameron had his guard up again and didn't respond. I liked conversation, especially about school. Lunch in particular. Fish sticks, taters and gravy, tater tots, pudding, peanut butter cookies, milk, even cold chicken legs. It didn't matter to me. I'd eat my helping and anything my classmates didn't want to eat. Maybe Cindy would be in some of my classes.

"No, ma'am—Mrs. Daniels—the ninth."

"It's Miss Daniels, Ty. Please, call me Liz."

It wasn't in me to call her by her first name. That meant a licking at home or pulled ear at school.

Cameron and Mr. Jordan emptied the trailer, and I helped Miss Daniels stack.

"Ty, tell me about yourself. You live north of town. Any sisters?"

"No, ma'am, just my brother, Cameron there. I do have a dog, Jake, but he don't count as family. Then we have pigs, laying hens, and an old milking cow."

She grinned and placed a bale on the stack. "Oh, yes they do. You can love a dog, or any pet, just like family, and pigs are one of the smartest animals in the world."

Pigs didn't strike me as having much sense. Don't take much for smarts to wallow in the mud all day. "Well, yes, ma'am, I sure love my dog, but I don't know 'bout hogs."

"What does your mom do? Does she work?"

Cameron dropped a bale at my feet, took a deep breath, and broke in. "She ain't our ma. We call her Momma Ray 'cause that's what she wants. Our ma don't live around here."

Miss Daniels's lips turned down at the corners. "When's the last time you saw your mom?"

I had to think and looked to Cameron for help, but he shrugged and turned away. To be honest, I couldn't remember. It had been years, a lot of years. Time had slipped by without notice. All I could do was give her a shrug of my own. "It's been awhile."

We finished and me and Cameron loaded up. Standing around visiting with adults wasn't something we did.

Cameron waited until I closed the door. "They ask too many questions. What does she give two hoots about our family for?"

"She's just being nice. Not everyone in the world is

like Momma Ray and Dad."

"Yeah, well…"

Mr. Jordan hopped in, cranked up, and turned the air on high. "You men ready?"

Questions kept burning a hole in my tongue. "Mr. Jordan," I shifted in my seat, "you're a judge. Does that mean you put murderers and such in jail?"

Cameron coughed, put a hand to his mouth, and bent over. It sounded phony to me. I would have elbowed him in the ribs, but he got a pat on the back from Mr. Jordan. "You OK?"

Cameron raised and rolled his eyes at me. "Yes, sir, just got something caught in my throat."

"Ty, we don't have too many murders around here, small town and all. I haven't sat on the Bench for a murder trial in ten years. Most of it is just young kids making mistakes. A lack of guidance from moms and dads is mostly the cause."

We turned left onto Main and headed for the big highway toward Little Rock. "Mr. Jordan, I think we're going the wrong way," I said.

He turned on the left blinker, pulled into The Burger Stop, then looked at me and Cameron and grinned. "You think?"

17

The Burger Stop sat easy on my belly. A big ole burger with fries, a large soda, and an apple pie tasted better than anything I'd eaten in awhile.

My eyelids grew heavy. Cool air inside the pickup didn't help. I was ready for a good night asleep. I took a drink of soda that turned noisy, shook the cup, and held it up to see if any remained. There was never enough, even in a large cup, not for me.

Shadows had grown long by the time we turned off the road into the woods toward our house. It would be time to tackle chores.

"When I was a kid, I used to hunt coons out here," Mr. Jordan said. "Had me a couple of Black and Tans and boy, did I have a time."

He had my attention. "My Jake's a Black and Tan. He can howl the bark off a tree, I'll tell you."

"Yes, sir-ee. My old dogs could too. I got them as pups and called them Fred and Alice. My dad laughed and said I'd be the loneliest coon hunter in all of Arkansas. No one in their right mind would hunt with dogs named Fred and Alice. He may have been right, but I didn't care. It's been forty years since they passed, and I still miss them."

Cameron stirred. "Fred's a strange name for a coon dog for sure. Did you have a gun, or did you let your dogs have at them?"

"At first, we just treed them and kept count of how

many. I guess when I turned ten or eleven, Daddy gave me a single-shot, .410 shotgun, a break-over. I was proud as a strutting rooster carrying that thing around. Still got it too. I gave it to Randy when he turned eleven. I love the smell of burnt gunpowder. If I couldn't get them out-right with the gun, at least I could knock them out of the tree with a blast so Fred could have at them." Mr. Jordan's eyes lit and he smiled with big white teeth, excitement in his voice. "There's a hickory back of Parson's holler—we treed three coons in it at the same time.

"Yes, sir. You know, Fred nearly drowned in a creek back in there one night. Old coon got him under. Sure scared me. I was going to shoot, but you know how a scattergun is, might have shot my dog. Alice tried to help him, but I thought he'd bit the dust for sure."

I had the jitters like ants had crawled in my pants. "That's where Jake lost his eye, back of Parson's holler, chasing a coon. If I'd had a gun, well, I don't know. I didn't actually see the coon, but it scared me too."

"Yeah, you cried," Cameron said.

Sometimes, I wanted to poke Cameron in one of his eyes. Always quick to volunteer information about me and slow to open his mouth about anything he did or thought. He could jab my feelings with words, and it hurt more than an elbow to the ribs. He silenced me, ruined my story.

Mr. Jordan drove for a minute, quiet like. "Nothing wrong with crying, Cameron. Tears can wash away all the bad. I cried for my dogs when they died. I remember it like it was yesterday."

I put an elbow into Cameron and got one back.

We pulled in the yard and Mr. Jordan backed in

the trailer, by the barn, to turn around.

Our yard, house, and all the junk around it stood out in bright colors like I'd never seen it before. The sun might as well have been shining at high noon. Junky boat with a kitchen chair mounted in it, gray, weather-worn barn with holes in the walls and crooked doors, rusty pickup, a house with water-stained siding and dead leaves piled in the valley of the roof, tall weeds, and boards lying around. Shame coursed through me like a chill on a cold morning.

Mr. Jordan didn't act like he saw what I did. He pointed toward our barn. "That old Jake there, Ty?"

Jake stood just outside the door with his nose high in the air. "Yes, sir, that's him. You can bet he knew we were coming five minutes ago."

"I wouldn't take that bet, no, sir. Kind of askew with that eye gone, isn't he? Sleeps on the blind side too?"

"Yes, sir, but it don't bother him much. He gets along just fine."

Mr. Jordan bumped the transmission out of gear with the palm of his hand. "Men, here you go." He pulled two bills from his shirt pocket and handed one to each of us. "I really enjoyed your company today. You're good, hard-working young men."

Me and Cameron grew two inches in the seat. I unfolded the money, a fifty. Cameron got the same thing. I'd never seen that much before. Never. If my eyes were big as Cameron's, we must have looked a sight. Words left me again.

Mr. Jordan stuck his hand out and we shook. "I'm going to talk to your dad and see if you can work this weekend. I've got some fence that needs mending. Give you a chance to practice your driving skills.

Maybe Saturday, and Sunday afternoon after church. That OK with you?"

Cameron's face lit. "Yes, sir, it would be just fine with me." They locked eyes when they shook.

Good job, Cameron!

Jake stuck his head into the cab when I pushed open the door.

The back door on the house slammed and Dad stepped off the porch.

Mr. Jordan stopped Cameron. "Son, would you mind taking The Burger Stop sack and your cups and throwing them away for me?"

Uh-oh.

Cameron grabbed the trash, tucked the sack under his shirt and held the cups close, then backed away, walking at a quick pace for the barn. If Mr. Jordan didn't know, he did now. Maybe he wouldn't tell Dad we stopped and got something to eat. I counted on it, gave him a quick wave, and followed Cameron.

Cameron stuffed the sack and cups under a bag of chicken feed. "Dad sees that and we'll get what for. Can you believe how much money he gave us? The burger and fries would have been enough for me."

"Yeah, me too. Those cookies were good as I've ever ate."

"Like you're an expert on cookies."

"Cameron, quit cutting me. I know I ain't nothin' special. You don't got to keep reminding me. And let me tell my own stories too. You don't got to tell everyone about me crying over Jake."

"Yeah, you're right. Sorry 'bout that. Just jumps out of my mouth sometimes on its own."

"Well, stop letting your mouth get loose." I let that soak for a minute and continued. "I been thinking we need to find some more eggs to hide. Dad will be down to the doughnut shop tomorrow bragging 'bout that fish we caught. He might take Momma Ray, and we can eat good in the morning."

"I still can't believe you didn't take care of Dad when you had a chance. Wait. Be quiet. Where's Jake?"

Dad filled the doorway like he'd stepped from nowhere, a round peg in a square hole. "He give y'all money?"

Cameron and I answered at the same time. "Yes, sir."

"Give it here." He held out a chubby hand, spit on the floor, and took a step toward us.

I handed him the fifty. Cameron did too.

Dad took the bills and eyed us through his bifocals as he eased them open and pressed them against his pants leg. He rubbed each one between a thumb and forefinger like there might be more stuck to them. "He ask y'all a bunch of questions?"

Again, we answered at the same time. "No, sir."

"What'd you do?"

I took over. "Bucked bales and put them in a barn." He didn't need to know which barn or where. That would only produce more questions about Miss Daniels.

Dad spit again and disappeared, his voice lingered like the odor of a fresh cow patty. "Get your chores done and get to bed."

I walked to the door to make sure he was well away. "Cameron, that was close. You think he heard?"

"He didn't hear a thing. The thought of our money had him on a beeline to get it. He didn't wait around to listen to us talk 'fore he come in."

Jake walked back inside. I needed to pay closer

attention to my dog. He tried to tell me. I just missed it. "That pickup sure is quiet. I never heard it leave."

"T, this weekend, we got to figure out a way to ask Mr. Jordan to pay us in fives and tens, ones even, anything but a fifty."

I was missing something now. "Why?"

"Mr. Jordan didn't tell Dad we stopped and got something to eat. Dad didn't know how much money we got either. He'll never know if we squirrel some away."

18

I went to bed thinking about Mr. Jordan and woke up thinking about him. He talked about faith—a hope in something he couldn't see. A hope that the Lord would make his son well? Is that what he meant? Was he so sure in his faith he could go on with everyday life and be happy to boot? He said that's what it was, and he sure acted like it.

Is that what stopped me from trying to kill my dad? Faith that our life would get better?

It dawned on me that to have faith, you had to have patience—something I wouldn't know much about.

Most mornings started in turmoil. Dad's scream from the living room, "Get up, get up," followed by me and Cameron trying to hurry and dress and take care of personal needs before he opened the door to check on us. It never turned out good.

This morning, I woke before anyone else. I dressed and eased out of the house. When I pushed the kitchen door open, Jake sat on the step as if he'd been there all night waiting on me.

The morning felt great, cooler, not cool, but a good sign of fall taking a peek around the corner. Light dew covered the grass. A couple of chickens had picked a bush next to the house to roost under. The skeeters were still up, and some tried to take a sample from me.

I plopped down on the top step and put my arm

around Jake. He looked at me. I looked at him. "How'd you know it was me, boy?"

My voice started his tail to going.

"I wish you could talk and tell me how you know everything before it happens." He got a big hug. "I love you, my old doggie."

He had a bloody spot on one ear, but didn't flinch when I touched it, only ducked his head slightly, like it was sore. "What you been doing? You been out gallivanting at night without me? You better not be."

Jake's tail stopped and his ears twitched. Someone stirred. Was Momma Ray up to start the fire under the coffee? Jake eased out from under my arm and hopped off the porch. Dad coughed and a chair slid across the kitchen floor.

He looked up when I walked in. "Go get Cameron up. We got work to do."

Great, we'll have to choke something down on the way. The hay should be ready to bale. That might be his motive.

He missed the fact that I was awake and outside so early. He had a problem with Cameron being up and out early, but not me.

I shook Cameron. "Hey, wake up, we got work to do. Won't be feasting on eggs this morning."

"You don't know that."

"Yes, I do. Dad's up and raring to go already. And he ain't going to drink coffee and brag about fish neither."

Cameron stretched. "What'd he say?"

"Nothing, just told me to get you."

"That's about right. I'll be happy to see the school bus tomorrow."

"Yeah, me too. Come on before he stomps in here

screaming."

Momma Ray had a couple of biscuits with grape jelly set aside for us. We ate them on the way to the barn.

Dad waited on us. "You boys come on. We're going to load some hogs and take them to the sale this morning."

We'd loaded pigs plenty of times, but Dad always went to the sale alone, or Momma Ray went. Doing something new, like going back to town, would brighten the day.

Cameron perked up. "Where's it at, Dad? How long are we going to be there?"

"You ain't going. You got hay to bale. I'll drop you off on the way."

Cameron looked away, and his mouth moved with silent questions. He felt disappointed, I know, but who's to say? I thought he had the better deal, and if not for the risks involved, I'd suggest he went in my place. Driving tractor didn't bother me none. It made the day go by.

"While you boys were at old man Jordan's, I went and hooked up the baler. By the time we get back from the sale, you'll have bales ready for Ty to stack with the hay spear."

It struck me as Dad talked. He usually borrowed the neighbor's two-horse trailer when he had hogs to take to town. We built a little chute and pushed in the hogs. I didn't see it. "Dad, where's the trailer?"

"We don't need it. I'm only selling two. They're small. You boys can tackle them, and then we'll get a rope on them and put them in the pickup."

That's the craziest idea I'd ever heard. That old sow was going to eat one of us for sure. Pigs are low to the ground and strong as all get out. Even those shoats we'd been doctoring put up a heck of a fight, and they didn't weigh much at all. Dad sure didn't have it in mind to sell them. They weren't big enough.

Cameron looked like a fly buzzed around in his nose. He had a strong fear of pigs, even little ones that couldn't hurt you.

That's sure enough what Dad had in mind. He produced a couple of ropes and led the way to the sty.

When the sow saw us coming, she ran to the fence and rooted around by our feet, like she did at feeding time. This got the rest of the pigs excited. Flies took flight like a million geese leaving a lake all at once.

Dad pointed. "I want them two there—the white one with the split ear and that one with the black snout."

Holy cow! They were big as Dad.

"Just grab one by the foot and turn it over, just like you do the little ones. I'll tie their feet and we'll put them in the truck."

I edged over the fence, the long wooden slop trough at my feet. Cameron followed. I had my eye on the one with the split in his ear. My luck was running good because he walked up and nosed my leg. I pounced, grabbed a foot. *Look out.*

Dad screamed, "Get in there, Cameron. Don't stand there. Help him."

That hog kicked so hard my teeth chattered. I thought my arms were going to come loose at the shoulders. The thing squealed and ran three-legged, dragging me by his fourth leg through I-don't-even-want-to-think-about-what. There was no way I could hang on. It left me in the slop, spitting and sputtering, and then it scurried to the back of the pen. Rolling, I got to one knee.

Dad struck with his big, tooth-loosening right fist, and Cameron landed flat on his back under the old sow.

19

Cameron sat on the edge of the seat. Any closer to the door and he'd slide off in the crack onto the floorboard between the seat and the door. We had a tooth just alike now, both of them loose. I noticed him rubbing his tongue across it. He'd been right about me leaving mine alone. It was getting better by the minute and didn't hurt much anymore. It would be better to mention that fact to him after he cooled off, maybe tonight.

Something had lit a fire under Dad this morning. We sailed down the road to our pasture. Stretches of washboard road pulsed through the seat, all the way to Dad's belly and my cheeks.

Dad turned into the hayfield and stopped next to the baler. Cameron had the door open before we stopped. He got out and slammed it.

Dad yelled through his open window. "Hey, boy! You better get over it! I'll give you some more if you're not careful."

Cameron stopped, but he didn't turn.

"Don't get in a big hurry to finish and plug up. It's an all-day job. We'll be back in a bit."

I looked back before we topped the first rise. Cameron's tractor coughed up a belch of black diesel smoke as he cranked up.

Driving through town, Dad slowed. The Burger Stop came and went on the right, Burger Monster on the left. I knew better than to ask how much farther. We were getting close. I could smell hogs.

The number of pigs assembled in one place at the same time was unbelievable. All the oinking and squealing, dust rising, and men hollering, I had never seen. Dozens of trucks and trailers were backed up to the pens. Wooden chutes of different heights, made to accommodate any sized pickup, truck, or trailer, stuck out from the pens. Men stood on fences counting and marking pigs with different colored paint as they streamed by. Orderly confusion.

Dad backed up to a gate and we got out. He waved a short, muscled-up man over. "I got a couple of hogs I want to get in the sale this morning."

The man spit and moved his chaw to the other cheek. "Well, go get 'em. The sale don't start for awhile yet."

Dad dropped the tailgate. "I got them here, just let me know where they need to go."

The man's eyes flew wide and he stepped over for a look into the back of the pickup. "Good grief!" He yelled over his shoulder. "Hey, Jim, there's a feller here with two tied up in the back of his truck!"

I wasn't the only one who thought Dad was nuts.

Dad took offense. If he'd been a hairy man, he might have looked like Jake, when my one-eyed protector had his hackles up. "You don't got to advertise how I haul a hog in here. You going to help me get them out of the pickup and sell them or not?"

"Yeah, sorry, but them two pigs are huge. How'd you get 'em in there?"

"This boy and his brother done it just fine."

The guy walked over to me, gave my shoulders a squeezing, and shook his head. "You and your brother must be tough, kid. I'll say that for you."

Bleachers and benches lined the walls on three sides of the sale barn, like the ballpark in town. Dad picked a spot high enough for us to see into the arena and plopped down.

He leaned over and whispered in my ear. "You sit here and don't you move."

"Why, where are you going?"

"I ain't going nowhere. You just listen. Don't scratch your ears, touch your head, or pick your nose. Don't move."

"Yes, sir." My nose started to itch just because he'd said don't touch it.

A man dressed in a white shirt with a black string tie, black pants, and cowboy boots walked onto a small platform above the pens with a microphone. A gate opened at the far end of the arena and a group of pigs scurried in and milled about. One or two rooted in the sand and rolled. All of them had red letters and numbers on their backs.

Speakers in the rafters blared and the auction began. The auctioneer had his own voice. He sang a song you could tap your foot to. Each bidder, like our music teacher at school with her stick, could change his tempo with a nod of their head or a short wave of their hand. "Who wants to give me seventy, now seventy, seventy, got seventy now seventy-five, eighty, where's eighty-five, now ninety?" Then, with a sudden scream, "Sold!" Gates swung open, the pigs exited to the left, and another group entered from the right.

The song began anew.

I saw why I didn't need to pick my nose. Dad didn't want me to buy a pig by accident.

The men who handled the sale were something to

watch. Those who moved the pigs in and out of the arena carried sticks or short pieces of plywood. Pigs reacted well to the pressure of the stick, moving this way and that way about the arena, with just a push on the shoulder or jab in the hip.

Miss Daniels might have been right about hogs being smart. They sure looked easy to train.

I was going to get me and Cameron sticks to use. This looked too easy. I was trying to decide what tree I could cut on when Dad leaned over and elbowed me.

He stared into the distance, toward the opposite wall. "Boy, I'm going to the truck. You sit here and watch for our pigs and listen to what they bring. Come tell me, you hear?"

Stunned, words fled me.

He stood up and left, disappearing around the corner before I thought to protest or ask for advice. What in the world was he thinking? All I knew about pigs could be summed up in their smell. I hadn't even learned the auctioneer's language yet, and he wanted me to listen and report. I'd been somewhat comfortable listening and learning. Now my nerves stood on edge.

Pigs came and went, black on white or white on black? Hard to tell which. Red and white, all red, all black, flat noses, the oinks all the same.

One of ours had a black snout and white body. The other had a black rump, white front but a split ear. Or was it the other way around? All white with a split ear, or black snout and white body with a split ear? The harder I concentrated the more confused I got and the more they looked alike.

To add to my burden, I realized I was the only kid sitting among men. I looked around to see if they watched me, but the goings on in the arena had their attention. I shook myself and focused on the pigs. I didn't want to mess up.

Pig, after pig, after pig, then, finally, I thought I recognized one. I listened to the auctioneer as the numbers spewed from his lips. Now and then I recognized a word. Numbers, I needed numbers. There they were. I picked some and ran for the pickup.

When I opened the door, Dad leaned over, turned the radio down, and looked at me. When I told him what I'd heard, he grinned. "That's good, that's a good price, boy."

Just before noon, he went into the sales office to get his check. I didn't think much of it until he stomped back to the pickup and jerked the door open. "You give me the wrong figure. They sold for ninety-two cents, not ninety-five. You got to be the dumbest kid in Arkansas."

It was too good to be true, and I knew it. There's no pleasing him. And what difference did it make anyway? Three cents a pound on a two-hundred-pound hog? Even with my limited ciphering skills I knew that wouldn't buy a small burger at The Burger Stop.

We drove to the hay pasture.

Cameron had two-dozen round bales rolled, plenty for me to get started stacking.

Before I got out of the truck, Dad stopped me. "Here, share with your brother." He gave me a bottle of water and two cans of Vienna sausage.

I wondered where the crackers were. Better than nothing.

"Thanks, Dad. I will."

"Stack them bales where you always do. One on two on three, got it?"

"Yes, sir."

The hay spear was four feet long, two inches in diameter. A big skeeter's beak mounted on the front of a worn-out tractor. I'd be able to spear the center of the round bales, carry them across the field and stack them.

I cranked up and drove out to give Cameron his lunch.

He stopped and got off. We met in the middle, between our tractors.

"How was your *hog* sale?"

"Hey, it wasn't my choice to go with Dad. He picked me. You can be his favorite anytime you want. I'll come out here."

I worried about Cameron. He and I were twins, but our hearts were as different as our looks. Cameron's heart got harder by the day.

"It wasn't a big deal anyway. A million pigs for sale, that's all. The auction guy confused me, talked too fast. He spoke English but sounded like he had rocks in his mouth. You know what's crazy? Dad told me to listen to what our pigs sold for then walked out, left me sitting there alone. He sat in the pickup, listening to the radio."

Cameron thought on it a minute. "He felt uncomfortable. I'll bet you. That's why we live so far out in the woods. He don't want folks around to witness his goings on. That's why he left. He feels like everyone is watching him."

"I felt the same way, sitting there by myself. Oh, here." I reached into the hip pockets of my britches and handed him a tin of sausage and the water bottle. "I ate mine and drank half the water."

"Where'd you get these?"

I nodded toward the road.

Cameron shook the water bottle like he couldn't believe it had anything in it. "You're joshing me."

"Nope. How's your tooth?"

He gave me his Scrooge look, but kept his tongue.

"Cameron, you OK?"

"No, I'm not OK. One of them pigs stepped in my mouth. You know what they wallow in, don't you? And look at my tooth." He pulled his lip up.

"Cameron, you forget I got one, too, just like it? We've been hit before. A whack's a whack."

"This is different." He pulled the tab up, peeled back the lid, and dug out a sausage.

"How do you figure?"

"I used to think it was my fault 'cause I got the fire beat out of me then worked my tail off to please him." He chewed and talked around the sausage, smacking. "Now, I know better. There's no pleasing him. He's evil and does it 'cause he likes it."

Cameron had a good point. I shrugged. "What do you do?"

"I'm thinking I might find a way to free us myself."

20

Cameron tossed and turned under the covers like a coon trussed up in a tote sack. The last time he kicked he got a toe into my calf and ended my sleep for the night.

Dad hadn't come for us in the hay field until after dark. Then there were chores to do. We went to bed with a half moon straight overhead, but now, it was out of sight and blacker outside than Momma Ray's flame-burnt coffeepot. First light and the first day of school wasn't too far off.

The school bus stopped at the end of our road, a fifteen-minute walk, but I didn't mind, at least not in nice weather. But when a sure enough storm roared through, it could be a bugger.

A fly traveled the room, its buzz only interrupted when it hit a wall or bounced along the ceiling. It sounded sick, louder than most. Irritating, like one drop of water after the other, *ker-plunk*, dripping in a puddle outside the window after a rain. Every time it journeyed toward the corner where the sticky strip of yellow flypaper hung, I hoped it'd be its last trip.

Outside, Jake snored with steady, hard breaths in short puffs.

I'd miss Jake come winter when he'd sleep in the barn on a pile of burlap sacks. It was nice to know he stood guard outside the window.

Cameron kicked the tar out of me and screamed.

He jumped straight up, and I jumped with him. His white body, easy to see in the dark, moved quicker than I could react. The next thing I know, he had me penned against the wall, gouging my belly with his fists.

I wasn't the one who needed holding. He'd gone crazy.

"Cameron, Cameron, wake up." I gave him a good whack on the side of his head with my open hand and ducked out from under him.

Jake whined.

I kept my hand on his back, held him against the wall, and shook him. "Cameron, you had a nightmare. You OK?"

He whispered between breaths. "I thought, I thought that old sow got me down and was eatin' on me. It was real as anything, T." He wiped his face. "I'm soaking wet and my heart's beating fast as a rabbit's." He sucked in a deep, long breath. "Did I scream?"

"Like a girl."

"We ever get out of here, Brother, I'll never own a hog. I hope I woke up Dad."

"You do? Well, we'll know soon enough. I hope Momma Ray got us some new pants and shoes."

"Me too."

Jake shook himself. His ears flapped like a covey of quail taking flight.

Cameron kind of laughed. "If she didn't, my ankles will be cold this winter."

"You see light coming behind the oak yet?"

"Yeah, won't be long."

I bent and pulled on my britches. "Let's get chores done. I'm ready to go to school. Maybe Dad will stay off his high horse. I'll feed hogs this morning."

"You're ready to see Cindy."

"Cameron, don't be—"

"I'm sorry. It jumped out 'fore I could stop it. Thanks for tending the hogs. I'll be out in a minute."

Jake acted strange and didn't appear to be his usual self, looking for hugs and scratches. He pulled away when I tried to hug him and pointed his nose down the road, smelling the air. "Jake, the sun ain't even up all the way. No one's coming. Come on, boy. How's your head? Let me look at it." He didn't flinch when I rubbed the spot. "School starts today. Course you wouldn't care about that, but I won't be home until afternoon. You'll be on your own."

The slop bucket didn't have much in it, but we were two pigs fewer now. While the water trough filled, I got a bucket from the barn and filled it with some terrible smelling stuff Dad got in town to feed them. Never seen anything a pig wouldn't eat and like. The nastier, the better.

Jake padded off toward the barn. I shut off the water and followed him. Cameron had made it out to help.

"Cameron, what are you doing?"

He stood like a statue, feed can in one hand, head cocked to the side. Jake stood next to him, ears and tail up.

"Cameron, what's the matter?"

"Shush, someone's out there."

"Out where? In the woods? Who'd be out there this time of morning? There ain't no one out there. Jake would be howling."

"Shush don't mean ask a bunch of questions. Listen a minute, I felt someone looking at me."

"Cameron, you can't feel a look."

He straightened and let his shoulders sag. "Don't tell me you can't feel Dad looking at you."

He was right. I felt Dad's stare. It was like the first sniffles, when you knew a cold was coming on.

"You sure it wasn't Jake watching you?"

Cameron turned huffy. "It wasn't Jake. He's right here looking the same direction. He feels it too. Come on, let's go see."

I had my doubts now. Cameron might be hearing or feeling things, but not Jake. Something had his attention.

"Maybe we should take a stick. Just in case. I'll get the broken shovel handle."

"Come on, Ty. Don't be a weenie. It's probably just some coon hunters traipsing through the woods looking for the road. We're looking for eggs as far as they're concerned."

"Yeah, well, we need eggs. You got anymore hid you ain't telling about?"

Cameron grinned. "I ain't telling."

We spread out, checking the usual places. The Bantam liked a thick, thorny bush growing at the corner of the barn. Two big, white hens liked each other's company and roosted together inside an old tractor tire in the weeds, cackling back and forth.

Cameron wandered farther away from the house than I felt comfortable going, now that the thought of someone lurking nearby had hold of my imagination. He had seven eggs in no time.

"T, come over here and look at this."

"Look at what." I trotted over, expecting to see real proof.

Cameron kneeled and pointed to a mark in the

dirt. "That's a boot print." He traced it out with his finger.

"That don't look like a boot print to me."

Cameron stood and placed his foot in it. "See? Almost the same."

"Yeah, now it looks like a shoe print."

Jake pointed his nose straight up, grabbed on with his toenails, and let a howl loose that stood all the hair up on me, plumb down to my ankles.

My imagination ran away then. No one ever came around our house. Mr. Jordan was the first one to come around in I couldn't remember when. Course we spent a lot of time in the hay field, away from home, but Dad and Momma Ray didn't have folks come for dinner, and me and Cameron sure didn't have friends over.

It had to be coon hunters. Didn't it?

Dad screamed for us from the front porch.

"Cameron, we going to tell Dad someone had been out here?"

"Nah, I'm not. He'd think we're crazy. You find some eggs? Eggs are a good excuse to be out in the woods."

I showed him the four I had.

Momma Ray had a real treat ready—pancakes. I couldn't remember the last time we had pancakes and honey.

We found a new set of school duds on our bed.

I peeled off what would be my chores clothes from then on, grabbed the first pair of pants I saw, and ripped off the tags.

Cameron held up his. "Look at these. Who'd she think she was buying clothes for? It wasn't for skinny hillbilly kids, that's for sure."

He slipped them on, and I laughed long and hard.

He pulled them as high as he could and still couldn't get his toes out the ends of the pant legs.

"And look at this," he said, holding a shirt for me to see. "Two red, two red and white checkered, and two brown. Let me see, one checkered and one brown are mediums. What do you think is so funny? What am I going to do with these britches?"

"You can trade me for these baggy things." I held a pair to my waist. They were the right length, but made for someone with meat on their bones. "She bought for twins, but didn't get the same sizes. What color shirt you wearing?"

"I don't know, why?"

"You want to wear the same color?"

"No, I don't. Let's draw straws."

"I ain't drawing straws. Just pick a color. I'll wear something different."

Cameron picked the checkered one and slipped it on.

"Cameron, we're going to have to treat these britches like riding next to Dad in the pickup."

Cameron grabbed a box and dumped out a pair of black tennis shoes. "How do you figure that?"

I fed my belt through the pants and pulled it tight. Like the drawstring in the top of a sack of onions, the material folded around my waist between the belt loops. I turned a slow circle to show him. "I'm going to wear these today. Tomorrow, it'll be your turn to look dumb."

21

Cameron had something on his mind. We no more than left the house and he'd out walked me by twenty paces.

Jake trotted between us, altering his course to sniff about and mark a bush now and then.

I always wondered how Jake knew where to piddle. What was he smelling? Another dog? I'd never seen dogs around, and Jake never howled like he smelled any close to the house.

"Cameron, slow down. My feet are killing me. These shoes 'bout got the end of my toes rubbed off already. I'll have to cut the ends out of them before the year is over."

"Come on. We don't want to be late for the bus the first day."

"You act like you got a girl you want to sit next to."

Cameron spun to walk backwards. "I can sit next to all of them. Don't bother me none. Except that girl, Misty. She asks too many questions."

I didn't mind questions when girls asked them. Unless it was a girl teacher looking for answers to school stuff. I didn't like that much. "What kind of questions?"

"You know. What's your favorite color? Do you like dogs? What did you watch on television? Do you like me? Just dumb stuff girls always ask."

"We don't watch television."

"That's what I told her. She didn't believe me."

"Do you like her?"

Cameron shrugged and turned to walk forward. "I don't dislike her." He spun back around. "You think she meant it, like boyfriend stuff, when she asked if I like her?"

"Could be, Cameron. No telling what a girl is thinking. I been pondering them lately and ain't come to a decision. You could have gone for a soda pop."

"T, you are so funny, pondering girls. Yep, you're real funny." He spun again.

I grinned at his back. It was nice to gig him for a change.

"I wonder what's for lunch today," I said. "I'm sure glad Momma Ray stopped at the school and signed us up for the lunch program. Might as well eat sawdust when she makes our lunch."

Cameron skipped one time. "Don't care what it is. I'm going to eat it."

Another kid waited at the bus stop when we got there. He stood a head taller than me and Cameron—big to be on the same bus with us. Earphones plugged his ears. Gray wires ran down to his bulging shirt pocket. The toe of his white tennis shoe tapped the gravel to a beat I couldn't hear.

I smiled at him and said, "Hi," but he didn't pay us no mind.

Jake put his nose to his leg and gave him a sniff. He looked down, shook his leg and Jake let him be.

Cameron nodded at him. "Kind of reminds you of Randy Jordan 'fore he got sick and lost his hair, don't he? Kind of uppity. I wonder what's stuck in his craw."

"There's no telling, Cameron. Maybe he just likes

his music and don't want to be interrupted. Dad ought to get him one of those things. We wouldn't have to listen to his old country whining all the time. Must be one of them players everyone has."

Cameron eyed the kid up and down and talked loud, like he didn't care if he heard or not. "Got to be a new kid. I don't remember him from last year."

The squeal of brakes echoing through the woods sounded familiar, the bus picking up the Thompson kids just over the hill. After a minute, it lumbered into view, a yellow beast trailing a cloud of black smoke.

Mrs. Adams, the driver, found someone to fix her blonde hair for her, or she got up early enough to do it herself. Most times she looked like she slept with her head under the pillow, jumped out of bed and got in the bus. She'd pulled it back into a braid and even had on a smearing of red lipstick and eye stuff, black and thick, with a shade of blue on her eyelids.

She was all business and didn't put up with nothing. "Good morning, boys. Come on, we don't got all day. Take a seat, we're running behind."

I gave Jake a pat on the head. "You go on home, boy. I'll see you this afternoon."

Cindy sat toward the middle of the bus. John Hillman, a kid who fancied himself a cowboy sat with her. She smiled. I gave a little wave and sat down in an empty seat that matched my heart. My day was ruined.

Cameron started to sit in the seat across the aisle from me, but the new kid pushed by him and sat down in it himself, as if he owned it or something.

Cameron looked at him and sat next to me. "You believe what he just did?"

"Just leave it be. Don't get in trouble."

My brother's jaw flexed. Not a good sign.

The kid removed his earphones, turned, and stretched his legs across the seat, so no one could sit next to him. The next group of kids had to push by his feet to get down the aisle.

He eyed me and Cameron. "Looks like you two just got them clothes out of the package and put them on. Stupid looking if you ask me."

I looked straight ahead, Cameron too, but I knew it wouldn't last. If the kid didn't keep his mouth shut, there was going to be a down-home fist-a-cuffing.

"Don't you hillbillies …?"

Uh-oh, the fuse was lit now. Cameron and the kid stood at the same time.

Mrs. Adams screamed, "Hey!" She knew what would happen next. She slowed and pulled over to stop.

Cameron spoke calm, like he was talking about everyday things. "Take it back."

"I'm not taking nothing back, *hillbilly*." The kid stuck his nose out and made a show of sniffing. "Why don't you take a bath before you come to school? You and your brother stink. I smelled you five minutes before you got to the bus stop."

"Take it back."

The kid hit Cameron square on the nose. The smack silenced the bus. You could have heard a mouse squeak. Not a kid moved. Even Mrs. Adams stared at them. The first time I remember her tongue getting stuck in her mouth. She always had something to say.

Cameron never blinked. Then he done something I couldn't believe. He smiled and said, "Is that all you got?"

Cameron went nuts. Blood and screaming the likes I've never seen. The bus erupted in yells. Mrs. Adams ran back and tried to pull Cameron loose, but she'd pull and the kid screamed all the more. His ear stretched, long and thin. Cameron had the lobe between his teeth and wouldn't let go.

I finally got hold of Cameron and yelled in his ear something about Dad going as nuts as he was when he found out he'd been fighting.

Cameron spit him out, pushed away, and shook me off. "Let me go."

Mrs. Adams unloaded on him. "Cameron Ray, you sit in that seat and don't you move." She guided him by the shoulders and pushed him into the seat behind me, next to another kid I didn't recognize. The boy moved against the side of the bus like *crazy* was a disease he could catch.

The big kid held his ear and moaned, rocking back and forth.

"Son, what's your name?"

"Jason, Jason Morris." He pointed at Cameron. "He's crazy."

Mrs. Adams stomped and screamed, "Enough, all of you! Be quiet! I don't need this on the first day of school. You two." She pointed at Cameron and the other kid, Jason. "Don't you move, not a twitch out of ya, you hear me?"

Cameron was cool as anything. He acted like nothing had happened. He even shrugged and raised his eyebrows.

I whispered to no one, to anyone, "We're in big trouble."

Mrs. Adams spun and pointed her red fingernail again, right in my face. "That means you too. Don't say a word."

Just behind Cameron, Cindy's face came into

focus. She mouthed, "Be quiet," and put a finger to her lips.

22

Mrs. Adams pulled to the curb in front of the school, shoved the lever to open the door, and stood to face us. "All right, have a good day. Cameron, you and Jason keep your seats.

"Ty, you can go to class. You didn't do anything wrong."

"No, ma'am, I'd just as soon stay with Cameron."

"Suit yourself. You'll be counted tardy if you don't go."

Being counted tardy was the least of my worries.

Everyone took a good look as they filed down the aisle and out of the bus. Cindy gave me a grimace, then followed it with a weak smile. I almost changed my mind and followed her. She might ask me some questions. If I stood close enough, maybe a whiff of the flowery stuff she splashed on would come my way.

Some kids ran to the front of the school. Small groups formed and they pointed, blabbing about what they'd seen for sure.

I'll say one thing for Cameron. He got the big boy to keep his trap shut. Just stared at the floor and never uttered a word about us stinking hillbillies. I couldn't blame him none really. After what I saw, I wouldn't want Cameron biting on my ear neither.

Mrs. Adams parked the bus and led us to the principal's office, a dreadful place. The front office was one thing. The ladies were nice, even when they gave you a tardy slip. And that's where they announced over the loudspeaker what was for lunch. The microphone stood on the head-lady's desk.

The office no one wanted to enter was in the back. The door into that place was closed. It was like looking into the woods in the dark of night, wondering about the noises—scratching and breathing and eyes looking at you that you couldn't see. Who knew what went on in there?

The door was closed, so maybe someone besides Cameron was in trouble. Maybe the principal had to go somewhere. Could we be that lucky?

People gawking bothered me. They couldn't mind their own business and go about their chores. One lady, when Mrs. Adams told her what happened, puffed up like a sitting hen, like her kid got the licking.

Mr. Ellis's deep voice followed a stamping of feet, "No running in the hall," just before he walked in and gave me and Cameron a quick eye. His walk and smile reminded me of Mr. Jordan. He had on a blue suit with a white shirt and yellow tie. If he hadn't been the principal, I might have felt comfortable.

After a brief conversation with Mrs. Adams, he looked in our direction. "Gentlemen, would you come with me, please?"

Jason jumped to his feet first. I knew he was going to open his mouth just as quick as he could. "Sir, do you know what he—"

A quick, firm hand waved and cut him short. Mr. Ellis opened the door to his office, "Please sit." Then he used the same hand to offer us one of the four chairs in front of a large wooden desk.

Me and Cameron took a seat, leaving the empty chair between us and Jason.

To our left, nice, neat frames with fancy writing hung on the wall next to a piece of white notebook paper with a stick-dog, a smiley face, and *i luv DAD* written in blue crayon. Below, a frame with a picture of a lady and three kids stood on the corner of a smaller desk, to the right of a computer screen.

Mr. Ellis took his seat and folded his hands on top of the desk. "All right, young man, you're new. I'm Brett Ellis. What's your name?"

"Jason, Jason Morris. This guy is plum crazy and he—"

"Whoa." Mr. Ellis held up both hands this time. "Slow down, and give me the facts. Tell me exactly what you said and did, nothing more."

Jason clammed-up and never said a word. His face turned red. He just sat there like a bump on a pickle.

Mr. Ellis looked at Cameron. "Mr. Ray. What did you say?"

"Take it back."

"Excuse me. Take what back?"

"He said we were hillbillies and needed to take a bath before we came to school. Said we stink. He could smell us five minutes 'fore we got to the bus stop. I told him to take it back. That's all I said."

"What did you do?"

"I stood up."

Mr. Ellis's eyes flashed to Jason, but the kid wasn't looking now. Not so eager to open his big mouth neither.

"How did the fight start? Ty, you want to tell me, please? Did you get involved?"

"Me? No, sir. This kid hit Cameron square on the nose, but Cameron laughed at him. I didn't do a thing because it was a fair fight, one on one."

Mr. Ellis eyed the three of us. Then he grinned at Cameron. I had something to hope for in that smile, because if he called Dad, our goose was cooked.

"Mr. Morris. I'm going to give you some advice. These hillbillies, as you called them, work. They do chores, cut wood, buck bales, tend hogs and cattle, no telling what else. I hear you got a licking, but you don't look too much the worse for wear. You got Cameron by twenty pounds and six inches and hit him on the nose first. I suggest you keep your mouth shut and keep your hands to yourself. I'm going to leave this among us men this time. I better not hear of another incident. Go to class. Now, go on and welcome. You have nothing to prove here, you understand?"

The kid's head couldn't have gotten lower and stayed attached to his shoulders. "Yeah," he said.

"Mr. Morris. 'Yes, sir'. Not 'yeah'. You'll find it's 'Yes, ma'am' too. Save yourself some embarrassment and use it from the start. Off you go."

"Yes, sir."

Cameron and I stood, but Mr. Ellis held us with a headshake.

"Please close the door behind you, Mr. Morris."

When that big door clicked closed, my heart jumped up there in the back of my throat where Dad kept it all the time. I thought we'd got off free and clear, but now I wasn't so sure. To add to my feelings of dread, the bell rang for school to start and we were tardy.

Mr. Ellis hemmed and hawed once and cleared his throat. "Men, I need to give you some advice too. How do I say this? You're getting to the age where your bodies are starting to change. Well, do you know what deodorant is? Do your mom and dad...have they bought you some to use or suggested that you use some?"

Cameron looked at me like "What?" I couldn't fathom what in the world he was talking about.

"Mr. Ellis, I'm afraid I, we," Cameron indicated me, "don't know what you mean."

"Boys, it's for body odor."

I could only think of one thing. "Well, sir, Momma Ray keeps baking soda in the icebox, but she told us to leave it be."

23

The paper Mr. Ellis gave me to get into class felt nice in my hand. I had an excuse, a good one and from the man himself. I stepped light. It could turn out to be a good day after all.

Me and Cameron checked our schedules. We didn't have one class together. Brothers weren't supposed to sit in the same room during school, or so it seemed.

My schedule would sour milk. Math, then science for my first two classes and they were my worst subjects. Miss Betty Sue, the math teacher, was famous for her tests and her sense of humor. Humor I liked, but tests were sure to give me trouble. Dad didn't like C's, and D's would get the tar beat out of you.

Miss Betty Sue stopped mid-sentence, and heads turned my direction when I walked in the room. So many eyes trained on me made my baggy pants, cinched belt holding them up, and wrinkled shirt all the more uncomfortable. Tomorrow, Cameron could wear this stuff.

Cindy sat toward the middle of the row of wooden desks, close to an outside window, and next to her, smirk smeared all over his face, sat John Hillman—Mr. Cowboy himself.

Heat stoked deep inside me and pushed the blood up to my face, like the red stuff in the thermometer hanging outside our back door.

"Ty, are you going to stand there all day, or come in and join us?"

"Yes, ma'am."

"Yes, ma'am, you're going to stand there?"

The class snickered and got a look from Miss Betty Sue that could melt crayons.

Mr. Cowboy shook his head and glanced at Cindy. He made me want to poke him a good one on his right eye and bite his ear.

Miss Betty Sue took the excuse slip. "Thank you, sir. Please be seated."

Only two chairs remained and both of them were in the front of the class. Just right for the way my day was going. Miss Betty Sue wouldn't be wasting time. She'd jump into math ciphering right off, and I'd be the first one she'd see to ask a question.

I sat and Miss Betty Sue got on with it. "As I was saying, we'll begin the year…"

Class passed in a blur, without having to answer math questions, then science was next. By the time history ended and the lunch bell sounded, my belly moaned.

Cameron had his tray and sat with a couple of guys who lived down the road a piece from us. When I walked by, one of them mentioned coons. I could sit and talk about Jake and chasing coons most days, but I had my heart set on visiting with Cindy. She sat with another girl, Becky something, and had her own lunch she carried in a small, brown paper bag. Her mom made good sandwiches with real ham and cheese. Always had a box of raisins or a peach. She shared some with me once.

"Hi, Cindy."

"Hi, Ty."

Her voice, sweet as apple pie, had all of my attention. "Can I sit here?" I put my tray down and pulled out a chair. "Hi, Becky."

"Hi." Becky snapped her lips together and turned her shoulders away from me. She didn't want me to sit, but I didn't care.

Cindy placed her sandwich on the paper bag and put her hands in her lap.

Silence between us didn't feel uncomfortable with the rest of the kids clanking silverware and glasses and telling stories. Someone always talked too loud.

You'd think that no more words than I knew, they'd be easy to remember. Her green eyes made me forget even the little ones. I stared like it was my first time to sit next to her. She took a deep breath, put a hand to her cheek, near some freckles, and moved a strand of yellow hair. A golden heart earring rested on each lobe.

Her eyes darted to my left and above me. Mr. Cowboy walked up and plopped his tray down. He didn't even ask if he could sit at the table with us. Good thing for him he didn't, because I'd have told him he could sit in the parking lot for all I cared.

Cameron gave me a nod. He was done with the coon talk. He focused on lunch. Today was fish stick and tater tot day, with tartar sauce in a little paper holder. I didn't care for the sauce. Cameron liked it a lot.

I daubed mine with catsup.

Cindy ate like she talked. She took her time, one bite, hands in her lap—chew, swallow, then another bite. "Ty, how was your summer? Did you do anything?"

Her words were just for me.

"Well, not much. Work mostly, cut and baled hay." My mind went blank. "I went with my dad to sell some pigs." Oh, of all the things to say.

Mr. Cowboy jumped in. "That's not fun. That's work. What did you do for fun? Who would say they went to sell a pig? I went fishing with my dad, and we camped for a whole week. I caught a fish 'bout this big." He spread his hands apart, long as the lunch tray, his eyes locked on Cindy.

"Oh, I went fishing too," I said. "We took our boat down to the slough and put out a trotline with minnows on it. We caught a cat my dad said would weigh thirty pounds."

"You didn't either. No fish is that big."

Cowboy's tone came with the same smirk I'd seen in math class. He burned me to the bone and caused the blood to rise again until I could see red. "Yes, they do. I barely got it in the boat."

Cowboy shook his head and wrinkled his nose. "Un-uh, I don't believe it. We were going to go shoot my dad's deer gun. He had to load some bullets, but didn't get a chance. But we were going to."

Becky let out a big huff. Apparently, boy talk wasn't to her liking.

I wouldn't mind having a gun to shoot coons with. One like Mr. Jordan gave to Randy. Wouldn't need a deer gun to do that. Just a little shotgun would work. Cowboy was trying to change the subject. "You weren't there and didn't see the fish."

Cowboy looked down his nose. "I been fishing my whole life and never seen or heard of a fish that big, not no catfish around here for sure."

"I worked for Mr. Jordan," I put in. Almost forgot that one. "He's a judge, puts bad folks away. We bucked bales and took them to a lady's house and unloaded them. We ate at The Burger Stop when we got through."

Cindy perked up when I mentioned Mr. Jordan, but Cowboy opened his big mouth before she could speak. "I picked up hay for Mr. Jordan. He's a good friend of my dad's. I didn't see you there."

"I was there, just two days ago, and I didn't see you neither."

Cindy picked at her food and glanced back and forth between us. Becky looked like she'd caught a case of the flu.

Then I threw in what I thought was sure to silence him. "Mr. Jordan taught me how to drive his pickup. Me and Cameron both."

"You're lying. He never did and you know it. Take it back."

Panic hit me. There was no way to prove I'd driven a pickup, or that Mr. Jordan had taught me. "You'll just have to take my word for it."

Hillman took a bite of fish and spoke, smacking his food. "I'm not taking the word of no storyteller. Take it back or I'm telling everyone you're a bald-faced liar."

It was all I could do to keep my hands to myself. Every inch of me begged to strike, but Dad didn't abide troublemaking in school. Said it made him look bad. Cameron might have already got us in a pickle.

Last winter, me and Cameron got creamed for fighting. My ears don't like cold weather because they stick out from my head too far and don't get any heat. At least that's what Cameron says. A kid thumped the right one while we were outside waiting for the doors to open to go into the school. Then, he laughed about it. I let it go, but Cameron seen him do it. A bad morning for thumper turned into a bad evening for us when Dad found out Cameron went crazy on the kid.

I stood and picked up my tray. I hadn't even finished the tater tots, the best of all. Cowboy kept mouthing off, rubbing the sore spot on my feelings. This turned out to be the worst day of my life.

24

Cindy sat two seats behind me, next to the window. Mr. Cowboy sat just behind her, on the edge of the seat, legs in the aisle. He ran on about his horse, a fifteen-hand tall roan, whatever that meant. Said his dad was teaching him to rope.

Like anyone cared two hoots. Big whup.

The screech of brakes drowned him out. The bus slowed. Mrs. Adams popped out the stop sign, opened the doors and another kid got off.

Cameron elbowed me. "What's the matter?"

"Nothing."

"You eat something at lunch that made you sick?"

"I'm not sick."

"You look sick."

"Cameron, sometimes you're thick as a tree stump. Leave me be."

He shrugged and eyed Jason, the kid who said he could smell us. His ear looked red, probably sore too. He hadn't been bumping his gums none. Bet he didn't go home and tell his ma and pa the neighbor kid jumped on him and bit his ear. Wouldn't blame him none because that wasn't a story I would tell. Too embarrassing.

Our stop came into view and none too soon for me.

Jake knew when school was out and waited for me at the bus stop. He never missed a day. He could brighten my worst moods. The urge to look back at Cindy only made the ache in my chest worse. Oh, Cowboy would be talking about me after we left. I just knew it. I kept my eyes on Cameron's back and followed him out the door.

"Hi, boy." Jake rubbed his head on my pants and tried to weave in and out between my legs, his tail going crazy. I gave him a scruff. "Come on, Jake, not now, quit."

Cameron kicked a rock down the road toward our house then looked back as Jason crossed in front of the bus. "He don't say much now, does he?"

Black smoke billowed and the bus pulled away. Sun glare on the windows prevented me from seeing if Cindy looked my direction. "Would you?"

"No, I don't suppose. Bet he ain't so quick to notice how folks smell no more neither."

That still bugged me. No wonder people looked at me. I took a quick sniff at an underarm but didn't notice anything unusual. "How we going to get deodorant to make us smell better? We don't have any money."

Cameron took a quick whiff of his own armpit. "I don't know. Besides a bath now and then, I didn't know we had to put something on."

"Dad and Momma Ray don't tell us nothing about stuff like that. And look at us, Cameron. They don't care about what we look like. I got to do something with these shoes. It's going to be hard to put my toes back in them in the morning. Might have to wear my old ones."

"Just tell Momma Ray they're too small. What can she do? You going to wear them all year?"

"Hey! Hey, wait a minute." Jason trotted in our

direction.

Here we go again. Going to be some more comeuppance for the big kid. I'll have to hit Cameron with a stick to get him to turn loose this time. Mrs. Adams was long gone.

Then something happened I never figured on. Jason stopped right in front of Cameron and stuck out his hand. "I'm...I'm sorry for saying what I did. I don't know why I said what I did."

Just like that. You could have pushed me over with a chicken feather.

I didn't have a clue how Cameron would react, but he took the hand, looked Jason dead in the eyes, and asked, "Friends?"

"Friends," Jason said.

Then Jason stuck out his hand to me. His grip was firm, his brown eyes direct, like he meant what he said. My smile only got a nod in return. He left the same way he came, trotting at an easy pace.

We walked for a spell, slow and quiet. There wasn't a thing to run home to. Cameron picked up a rock and whacked it with a stick.

"That took a lot of guts," I said.

Cameron shrugged. "Nah, I didn't think nothing of it."

"Not for you, goofy. For him. He did the insulting, got the whupping, then said he's sorry. That takes something, down here." I gave my chest a pat.

Cameron looked back at the empty road. "Might just be a big weenie, we'll see. So, what was your problem on the bus?"

"Oh, Hillman, ole cowboy wannabe, called me a liar at lunch."

"About what?"

"I told him and Cindy that Mr. Jordan taught me how to drive his pickup, and he said I lied."

"Why didn't you whack him? He'd take it back."

"Cameron, we can't be whacking everyone. Dad would have my hide and you know it. We might already be in trouble 'cause you chewed on Jason."

Cameron hit another rock and it whizzed off like a noisy bumblebee. "Nah, we're not in trouble. Mr. Ellis isn't going to tell. He said he would leave it in his office. I'm counting on it. Just forget what Hillman said. You didn't tell a lie. We know it. That's all that counts."

"Cindy heard and she's wondering about me now, all because of Hillman. She hasn't said a word to me since."

Jake stopped to look behind us. Dad's pickup rattled up the road with Momma Ray sitting in the middle next to him.

Cameron moved right, to Dad's side; me and Jake moved left. Dad stopped between us. "You boys are taking your sweet time getting to the house."

"Yes, sir," I said. "My shoes are too small and killing my toes."

Momma Ray leaned over to look. "You wear your old shoes tomorrow, and I'll take those back. You should have said something."

"Yes, ma'am."

Cameron stepped back from Dad's window as a stream of tobacco spit landed at his feet.

Dad wiped his lip. "Cameron, you have trouble with a kid on the bus this morning?"

Uh-oh, Cameron was in for it now. Mr. Ellis called after all.

Cameron never hesitated. "He said we smelled

and hit me in the nose."

Dad sat for a minute then turned off the pickup. He worked the chaw of tobacco and spit again. Water gurgled in the engine. Momma Ray put a hand to her mouth and coughed, quiet like, dainty almost. "The principal just said the boy insulted you. He hit you, eh? Did you hit him?"

"Sure, I hit him."

"I told you before not to cause trouble in school."

"Yes, sir, and I didn't cause no trouble. He did. I ended it. You want me to sit and do nothing?"

Cameron jerked and moved to the front of the pickup as Dad's door flew open, but he stopped and held his ground as Dad approached. Dad didn't move a muscle, Cameron neither, their noses only a finger's width apart, Cameron bolder than the cheek-lady.

Then Dad whispered, almost for Cameron alone. "When are you going to learn to listen and keep your mouth shut and not hit people?"

"You taught me."

Oh, Cameron, you shouldn't have said that.

Cameron never had a chance. Before I could blink, Dad grabbed him by the shirt and threw him on the hood of the truck.

The pickup horn blared, and we all looked into the cab. Dad, too. Momma Ray held it down for a good five seconds. Her lips were set, a thin line of red lipstick below rose-tinted cheeks and a white nose.

Dad froze, staring at her. She moved her head left then right twice, but not so much as to say quit. More of a warning to think before he hit Cameron. Dad turned loose, stepped back, then walked to the door to get in.

I couldn't help but notice Momma Ray slide over

against the passenger door. Got a little space between the lovey-doveys now. Not so happy. Cameron rolled off the hood, landed on his feet, and walked around beside me.

Dad hesitated at the door. "You boys ever think about running away? Do ya? I know these woods. I know people. You remember that." He opened the door, got in, and started up. "Get on home, get your chores done, and get a bath. You're going to church tonight, down to the little white church on the highway."

Me and Cameron stepped to the middle of the road and watched the tailgate disappear in the dust. Cameron straightened his shirt.

"That was real close, Cameron. You could have got killed for that."

"I'm not taking no more from him. If both of us stand up to him, he'll back down."

"I don't know about that. Did I hear him right? He's going to take us to church tonight? Do they have church on Wednesday nights?"

"I hope not. Maybe we can just mess around on our own, or run away." Cameron ran a hand over his head. "I don't believe he knows a thing 'bout these woods, and I ain't scared. Not no more."

"He'd kill us for running away."

"He'd have to catch us first, and he's fat, can't run no distance at all. How come he didn't come uncorked?"

"He did come uncorked. Momma Ray saved your hide, honking the horn like she did."

"Reckon she's found religion?"

"I don't think they go places where there's any to find. Besides, he could have given us a ride to the house, not made me walk in these shoes. I told him my feet were killing me. They might have found something, but I bet it ain't religion."

25

Dad had the radio turned up. Deep bass pulsed through the speakers, static in the background. The words were hard to make out.

I whispered to Cameron. "Your pits on fire? Mine are burning up."

"I thought it was just mine, and I scrubbed my pits good too. That don't help."

Dad turned down the lane to the little church. "What y'all whispering about? Quit whispering."

"Dad," I said. "That spray stuff burns."

"How much did you use? You ain't supposed to put on the whole can. It should last you a while. Just a quick squirt every morning's all you need."

Me and Cameron exchanged looks. Now he tells us. We couldn't believe they bought some. Should have told us how much to use before we put it on. Turns out, Mr. Ellis did us a favor after all.

Dad hit a button on the radio where another voice belted out a song. "You boys don't dally when the meeting's over. I'll be waiting on you."

He did a quick loop, pointing the pickup out of the lot, and stopped. We got out. The tires spit rocks at our feet when he left.

Cameron laughed in Dad's direction. "He's in an all-fired hurry to get out of here."

"Yeah, like to have hauled me back to the house with him before I could get out and shut the door."

We'd just been dropped in China for all I knew about going to church. People, families with mom, dad, and kids, women alone with books tucked under their arms, men alone, all walked toward the church like there wasn't a minute to spare. Not a familiar face in the bunch.

No suits, ties, or fancy dresses. Mostly jeans and tennis shoes, so we might fit in. I ran my hands around my waist, pulling up my britches.

Cameron tugged my elbow. "We ought to go hide somewhere, run off into the woods and skip this deal."

"We can't do that. You're the one who wondered if Dad would bring us to church after I told you what the lady at the bait shop said. Come on. Let's go see."

Cameron threw his hands out. "T, go where? See what? I just changed my mind and don't want to go in there."

I pointed. "The doors are open. People are walking through them. That's where. What's it going to hurt to go look?"

Piano music drifted on the evening heat, sweet and inviting.

"Hey, guys."

Jason walked up, his parents behind him. "Mom, Dad, this is Cameron and Ty. We, uh, we ride the bus together. They live down the dirt road across from the house."

I was shocked. Insulting us one minute and introducing mom and dad the next. His ear looked better, not as red.

Cameron's "hi" followed mine.

Mr. Morris offered his hand and we shook. "Men, pleased to meet you. Son, get on to catechism. We'll see you after church."

"Yes, sir."

The adults walked away leaving us standing there in the dirt. We looked at one another, all three of us poking the ground with the toe of a shoe, silent.

Jason spoke. "Do you guys know where to go?"

Cameron shook his head. "Haven't got a clue."

"Follow me. We don't sit in big church on Wednesday nights. We have something kind of like Sunday school."

My face must have given me up because Jason continued. "You don't know what Sunday school is?"

"We've never been to church," I told him.

"Really?"

"Really," Cameron said.

We stepped out with Jason in the middle. "What's cataclysm?" I asked.

"Catechism. It's like Bible study. Talk about God and stuff. Mostly just stories about people who died two thousand years ago. Y'all have a Bible?"

"Never seen one," Cameron told him. "Not that I know of anyway."

Jason led us up concrete steps through brown double-doors. Bright red carpet stretched wall to wall down a long entry and through another set of oak doors into a meeting hall that looked like it could hold two hundred people. Fifty, maybe sixty adults milled around toward a raised area in the front, shaking hands and talking. Some sat in long wooden seats with books in holders on the back of them.

Reminded me of school, girls and boys in separate groups. The piano struck up another tune, louder, the tempo faster.

At the end of the entry were three small rooms. In one, an older woman sat in a chair with a book on her lap. Four small kids sat on the carpet in front of her. In the second room, an older group of kids stood in a circle holding hands.

We entered a room like a big kitchen with a white stove and sink, brown cabinets, and gray tiled floor. A dozen white folding tables were stacked against the far wall, folding chairs next to them. One table and a dozen chairs were set up in the middle of the room.

A young guy who looked like he wasn't long out of high school spoke up. "If everyone will be seated, we'll begin."

Not what I expected for a teacher.

I recognized several kids from school. One boy, who was always quiet, kept to himself. He walked up and said hi and welcome. In school, he never said anything.

Me and Cameron sat next to Jason.

"Jason," the teacher said. "Would you like to introduce your friends to the group?"

I wondered what he would have thought if he knew there'd been a big scuff between friends on the bus that morning.

If Jason felt uncomfortable, he didn't show it. "This is Cameron and Ty, ah–"

"Ray," I threw in to help him.

"Cameron and Ty Ray," he finished.

"I'm Brother Mark. It's great to have you. Let's pray and we'll go around the table and introduce ourselves."

The next hour flew by faster than a night asleep. Before I knew it, we were praying again and then we were dismissed. Brother Mark never asked me and Cameron a question, as though he knew we didn't know anything. But then, I felt like he talked to only me. Like we sat alone, face to face. Before we left, he gave us our own Bible, a pocket-sized one with a red cover and the words *New Testament* in gold letters.

Jason's parents walked out with us. Mr. Morris pulled his car keys out of his pocket. "Do you boys need a ride home?"

Dad was nowhere in sight. "No, sir," I said. "Our dad should be along soon."

We said our goodbyes.

Another lady stopped to offer us a ride. We told her the same thing and then moved to one side, so folks wouldn't feel obliged to check on us.

The sun had set. Only a tinge of yellow glowed through the sky above the treetops, onto the back of some clouds, and made them glow with the yellow of a fire. The church, with its white board siding and wooden cross hanging below the steeple, stood out against the background of the dark forest.

The last light went out inside the church. After a minute, a small light over the doors clicked on. A man walked out and locked them.

The last car turned toward town and sped away, leaving us standing alone in the dark.

Cameron was quiet. It was unusual for him not to mention something, anything, about what he'd seen and heard. He was thinking, mulling it all over.

I couldn't wait for him to volunteer information. "What'd you think?"

"It was OK. They sure do lots of praying. Seems like it would be uncomfortable talking to a feller who ain't sitting there."

"You didn't pray?"

"Heck no. What would I say to Him? Like I said, uncomfortable talking to the air."

"Brother Mark talks to God like they're friends, and He's sitting there looking at him."

"He said God's everywhere. What's He look like, I wonder? I'd want to know what He looks like 'fore I'll talk to Him."

"I mentioned He was everywhere the other night. Don't know where I ever heard that. Maybe He's whatever you want Him to be, in your mind. I don't know." I looked toward the little building. "They had some pictures of Jesus hanging on the wall. He had long hair."

Cameron ran a hand over his head. "Well, they took that in the olden days. Barbers hadn't been invented yet."

"I suppose. Quite the story about that Joseph feller. His brothers selling him to them camel guys like they did. Then they lied and said he got killed. Their daddy cried."

"We ought to be in there. Mom sold us into slavery for a drunk and a job at a bar."

Sometimes Cameron had a way of making me feel let down. "I wonder where Dad is."

"Who cares? Let's walk. It can't be more than four, five miles at the most. Good thing you wore your old shoes."

26

Nighttime settled in black as roofing tar. Above, a sky full of stars twinkled in a moonless sky.

Rabbits, coons, skunks, possums, rats, mice and other critters went about their business, mostly rustling the bushes to make me wonder and quicken my pace. Meeting a skunk would be bad. It would take more than a squirt of deodorant to get rid of that smell. A flutter from a tree or the quick sound of wings on the wind told of a bird's travels.

I found myself behind several paces. "Sure not too many folks out this time of night, but I was thinking...we ought to hide if someone comes. Too many questions to answer."

"You're right. But what if it's Dad and we miss him? I know. We'll hide if they come from behind us."

I put my hand to my hip pocket to make sure my Bible was still there. "What did you do with your Bible?"

"It's in my pocket. Why?"

"Just wondering. You know it has red letters in it. I wonder why?"

"Not all of them are red, but some are. I seen it too."

"Reckon what they mean?"

A screech owl cut loose back in the woods. Irritating critters when they sat in a tree outside the window at night. They're good as any guard dog. The boogieman would have a screech like that if there was such a thing.

"Who knows," Cameron said. "I know what red letters mean on my tests and homework, but after that…I suppose we'll find out soon as we read some."

"Yeah, that's right. Didn't think about that."

Cameron let out a good puff. "I'm about ready for bed. How far we come you think?"

"Couple of miles maybe. The road down to the Thompson's house should be up here on the left. It's black out tonight. The white stripes are longer than I thought."

"Where'd that come from, T?"

"I don't know." I counted the paces from one end of a line to the next in my mind. "They seem shorter when we're riding in the truck. A car's coming."

We jumped into the borrow pit and ducked down. Just in time. Headlights topped the rise behind us. A pickup. Too quiet to be Dad's and coming from the wrong direction. The light grew brighter by the second. Shadows of grass and weeds grew bigger and darker on Cameron's face then moved quicker and quicker as the pickup approached. Then, just as fast, night returned. We stood to watch it speed away, two red lights with a small white light over the license plate between them. The air following it hit us in the back. It cooled the sweat and carried a hint of exhaust fumes.

"Look there, T. Jake's coming."

Sure enough, Jake padded up the road about sixty paces distant, illuminated for a second in the lights of the pickup.

He trotted straight to me, his tail going ninety. I gave him a hug.

Cameron bent over and scruffed him on the head.

"That's some dog. How'd he know where we were? He came right to us."

"Cameron, I already told you."

"T, you get out that red-covered book tomorrow and get to reading. If it mentions an angel named Jake, then I'll listen."

"I'm just saying. He knows everything. How else do you explain it?"

"Not going to try. Just a good dog looking for his master."

Uh-oh. Lights hit us. It was too late to run. Someone drove up on us while we talked. The glare of lights wouldn't let me see who, but I knew it couldn't be Dad. Jake's tail wagged, slow and easy.

The top of the car exploded in blue and red lights. May as well have been Dad because my heart reacted the same way.

A voice came from behind the lights, deep and husky but nice. "Boys, you're out walking the roadway late. Should you be hunting coons on a school night?"

I held up a hand to block the lights, but I still couldn't see past them. "No, sir, we're not coon hunting. We're walking home, that's all."

The headlights dimmed. Then the officer stepped into view. A dark man with no features. His gun, handcuffs, and the like, stuck out at his side—obvious with so much light behind him.

"Where you been?"

"Down to the white church for Wednesday night service," I said.

He walked up to us and turned, his face in the light. His pants had sharp creases down the legs, shirtsleeves buttoned at the wrists and creased like the pants. A neat, dark mustache curved downward beside his mouth. A cowboy hat shaded his eyes.

I watched his lips.

"You boys always take your dog to church?"

Cameron seemed happy to let me talk. "No sir. Dad took us, but he didn't come back when it was over. He said he'd be there, but I don't know...maybe something happened."

He leaned over to rub Jake's head and ears. "This your dog, then?"

"He's mine. His name is Jake. He came to meet us. Knew we were walking, I guess."

"I'm Sheriff Bowles. What are your names?"

"I'm Ty, Ty Ray. This is my brother, Cameron."

He pulled a small pad and pencil from his shirt pocket and scribbled in it.

"Well, I tell you what. You boys bring your dog and get in. I'll take you home."

Boy, we were in for it now. I felt like arguing, but what do you tell the sheriff? We crawled into the back with Jake between us. Jake sat in the seat, looking out the window like he'd done it before.

The car had a metal screen between the front and back and no door handles in the back. The radio squawked; it was a lady's voice. "Don and Willamina Ray, children Ty and Cameron, fourteen, no address, only a P.O. Box, no warrants."

Sheriff Bowles said, "Roger," into his police radio. "Point me in the right direction, one of you, please." His eyes appeared in the mirror. "Cameron, you're not much of a talker."

"No, sir," Cameron said.

I gave directions. Then I leaned over and whispered to Cameron, "What we going to tell Dad?"

"Let Dad tell the sheriff how come he didn't come

get us. We don't got to say a word. You watch."

Here it was again, plain and simple, laid out in Cameron's knack for stating the obvious. Simple always seemed to baffle me.

Our house loomed dark as the night around it. The living room light came on about the time the sheriff opened the door for us.

Jake hopped out and plodded off toward the barn.

Dad, dressed in khaki britches and white undershirt, stepped onto the front concrete steps. "What's going on here?" he yelled.

"I brought your boys home, Mr. Ray."

"Oh," Dad said. "Well, you boys go get your chores done and get to bed."

The sheriff's jaw dropped. "Wait a minute. You boys stay right there."

Cameron got it right again. Dad was in for it.

The sheriff pulled out a small flashlight, clicked it on and pointed it at Dad. Dad's hand flew up to guard his eyes. "Sir, I picked up your boys and their dog nearly two miles from here. They said you took them to church."

Dad walked off the stoop two steps and puffed up. "So? What of it?"

"You dropped them off and they were supposed to walk home? Four miles on a school night. Am I missing something, sir?"

"Well, I...I got truck problems."

The sheriff opened his mouth then closed it. He turned away from Dad, paused, looked into the night then turned back. "So, you go to bed and let them fend for themselves? Boys, step into the house. Never mind your chores for now. Mr. Ray, you step out here. I want to look you in the eye a minute."

27

We knew when the sheriff left. The walls shook with the bang of the front door slamming.

My Bible lay secure under our mattress. If Dad decided to vent his foul mood on us, I didn't want him to find it and take it away from me out of spite.

He never came to our room, but we heard his rant, venom muffled by walls and distance.

I knew better than to leave chores. "I'm going to go feed right quick."

"It's after ten, leave it for morning. I'm sleepy."

"I'm sleepy too, and tired from walking, but Dad would have at us and you know it. Besides, imagine you're an animal penned up with no food and water. I know Jake's hungry, and so am I for that matter. Momma Ray left pork chops and corn on the table."

Cameron perked up. "There's been a lot happening, but it's not like I forgot to be hungry. You're right, let's go."

We finally got to bed, and night passed before I got my eyes good and closed. Momma Ray stuck her head in our door to announce breakfast much too early for me.

I washed my face and gave my pits a good scrubbing and a squirt of deodorant before going to the kitchen.

Dad walked through about the time we finished an egg with toast. He never said a word. His pickup cranked up and left the yard.

He'd told the sheriff a big fat whopper last night. There wasn't a thing wrong with his old truck. He left us to fend for ourselves just like the sheriff said.

I made sure to put my Bible in my hip pocket before leaving for the bus stop.

A million questions floated in and out of my mind. We didn't get to hear all the story of Joseph. I wanted to know what happened to him. What happened to his brothers? They needed to get their hind ends warmed up for what they'd done.

I'd barely think of a question before another would pop in and replace it. I found myself looking forward to seeing Jason. He seemed to know about the Bible, or at least he knew more than I did for sure. He might have answers for me.

There had to be a way to get Dad to take us back to church. Working up the nerve to ask him was the biggest obstacle.

Jake led us down the lane to the bus stop. His tail moved left and right, not like a wag, but like a rudder, taking his backend with it to track first to one side then the other side.

"You know, T, you missed something last night."

"Like what?"

"Willamina, Momma Ray's first name."

"Oh, man, that's right. I thought I was hearing things."

Cameron's nose wrinkled as if the smell of a skunk had drifted through. "I bet she don't like her ma and pa for hanging that around her neck. No wonder she wants to be called Momma Ray."

"Yeah." I danced a little jig on the road. "Momma Willamina gotta get her purse 'fore she come to see ya."

It was dumb, dumb, dumb, but we laughed at it.

Cameron had a stick and was whacking rocks into the woods again. Each click of rock on wood was followed by an angry *whiz* as the pebble sailed away.

"Too bad we don't live in town. You'd be a good baseball player."

He hit another one to prove my point. "I wouldn't mind. I like it when Jimmy brings another glove, so we can play catch before school."

"Jimmy who?"

"Jimmy Thompson, down the road?"

"He plays baseball, in town? No kidding. I wouldn't have thought."

"Yep, sure does."

"We can forget baseball or any sport. No way we'll ever play."

Jake had his nose to the ground. A scent led him into the bushes. Maybe where a coon crossed the road.

Cameron bent to pick up another pebble to whack. "Hey, look at this." He dropped down and sat on his heels, one knee out to the side, elbows on his knees.

"What is it?"

"Looks like a motorcycle track. Turns into the woods right here. Jake's on it. See."

Sure enough. Someone had driven a motorcycle almost to the house then turned off the road.

"Let's see where it went."

"Cameron, we can't miss the bus."

"I know, we won't. Let's just look for a second."

Heavy dew covered the leaves and made the venture a wet one. We walked off the road no more than thirty paces and hit a dead end. No trail, just a wall of undergrowth.

"Cameron, this don't make sense. Who'd come park their motorcycle here by the house? I've never heard a motorcycle around here. Ever heard of a coon hunter riding one?"

"No, I haven't, but look at Jake. He's looking toward the house like whoever it was got off and walked that way."

"Yeah, but he's not letting on like it just happened. It's not fresh."

"Let's go to the bus stop. Maybe Jason has one. We'll ask him if he rode up this way."

"I got a bunch of stuff I want to ask him too."

"Like what?"

"About church last night."

Cameron quickened his pace, slapping the stick against his leg in time with each step. "I don't know about the Bible. I read some last night after you went to sleep. Lots of words like 'shalt' and 'doeth' and 'thee.' And stuff about living on words, not eating no bread. Bunch of skinny folks around in those days I bet, not eating and walking everywhere they went."

"You turned the light back on?"

"Yep, sure did. You drool and snore like Jake too. I never noticed you drool. Like sleeping with a dishrag."

"Cameron, what if Jason doesn't have a motorcycle?"

"I've been thinking on that. We're going to find out about that bike. Tonight, after chores, we'll take a walk and just see for ourselves who's hiding in the woods."

28

Jason walked up to the bus stop the same time we did. He had on a new pair of jeans, a blue shirt, a brown belt, and the same white tennis shoes.

"Where's your earphones?" I asked.

"It's not my earphones. I still got them. It's the cassette player. I had them on doing chores last night, bent over to scoop leaves out of a water trough, and it fell in."

Cameron laughed. "That'll do it every time."

"Sure will. It'll be awhile before I can save up enough to buy another one."

That surprised me. I glanced toward their place with its big red barn and brick house. "Your mom and dad won't get you another one?"

"No way. They give me an allowance. I save it, and if I want something, I have to buy it with my own money. They stopped giving me stuff—heck—I don't remember. A couple of years ago, I guess. Said I needed to learn the value of money. Besides, Dad warned me about doing chores with it in my pocket. I didn't listen."

Cameron looked him up and down. "You got to buy your own clothes too?"

"No, just play things, like the tape player, or if I want to go to the show, or a circus and the like. They have a disc player out and I might get one of those, but it's bigger, and I have lots of cassettes. I don't know yet."

"What's an allowance? Like…they pay you? I never heard of such a thing," I said.

"They give me twenty dollars a week for doing chores and helping around the house. I have to put some in savings. The rest is mine to spend or save or whatever."

Cameron laughed again but with no humor in it. "Our dad's on an allowance. We give him a hundred dollars just the other day."

Jason's forehead wrinkled, pulling his eyebrows together, but I broke in before he could ask what Cameron was on about. "Do you have a motorcycle?"

His face relaxed as his eyes lit. His voice went up. "I wish. Do you?"

I shook my head. "No, we don't have one neither."

Jason waved toward his house. "My mom is scared to death of them. Dad had one for chasing cows and wrecked it. He has a four-wheeler now. Why?"

Cameron pointed down our lane. "We found tracks by the house. Leads off into the woods, into nowhere, like it disappeared up a sweet gum tree."

"You know what." Jason held a finger up and shook it. "When we left for church last night, we passed a man on a motorbike. I don't know what color, didn't pay attention to it. Wouldn't think about it now except my dad mentioned how fast he was going. Said they were going to peel him off a tree one day. You think he went to see your folks or something?"

"No." I shook my head and scuffed a foot in the gravel. "This is different. First, we don't get people down to the house, and the tracks didn't go that far."

"Hey, T," Cameron nodded and motioned with his hand, "look who's coming."

Sheriff Bowles topped the hill in front of the school bus. He pulled over and stopped, holding up the bus, and lowered the window. "Good morning, men. Ty, Cameron, beautiful day."

Jason looked between me and Cameron without moving his head, and then he replied, "Yes, sir. Beautiful day. Yes, sir, it sure is." He hooked his thumbs in his pants pockets and shuffled his feet.

The sheriff pulled off his hat, put it on the dash, and ran his fingers through his crew-cut hair. The radio squawked and he turned it down. "Ty, are you and Cameron doing OK this morning? Did you get some rest last night?"

I looked at the bus and Mrs. Adams shaking her head, then back at the sheriff. "Yes, sir. We got some sleep after doing chores."

"Well, OK then. I'll be checking on you two. Stay out of trouble and tend to your school work." He looked across the road where Jake sat watching us. "I see your dog's keeping an eye on you."

Jason looked lost for words.

Cameron had words, just didn't feel the need to share them.

"Well, yes, sir," I said. "That's all he's got—one eye, I mean."

The sheriff reached for his hat and put it back on. He grinned and ran his thumb and finger down his mustache, one to each side of the mouth. "Ty, that's funny, real funny. Yes, sir, you're a funny kid. See you boys."

"Yes, sir, we'll see you." I gave him a short wave as the window went up.

Mrs. Adams stopped in front of us and the doors popped open. "So, now you got the sheriff looking in on you, eh, Cameron?"

"Yes, ma'am, we're real close. We like to visit quite regular. He was down to the house last night, come to mention it."

Mrs. Adams had on her old self, mussed hair, no lipstick, and a sour look, like she dipped her fair share from a jug of sour mash last night. She eyed Cameron close. The look caused him to hesitate in the door. "Come on, don't got all day. Quit your gawking and don't lollygag. Slow as molasses, you boys." She shook a finger at us. "I better not have any trouble out of you three today."

Cameron kept his attitude on the edge of being sassy. "No, ma'am. Me and Jason are real tight now, best of friends. Won't be no more trouble."

We shared grins. I sat down in the same seat with Jason. Cameron plopped down across the aisle.

Cindy wasn't on the bus, but Cowboy sat on his perch, legs in the aisle and watched with interest. He had on a straw hat that looked like a cow used it for a pillow. It fit his head crooked. The brim turned down in front, bent up in back, the sides curled like dried mud. Must store it in a shoebox at night.

He could go fly a kite. I knew the truth about learning to drive and wouldn't be trying to prove anything to him. Not no more.

Cindy was another story. One I couldn't get off my mind.

"Jason, you know a lot about the Bible?"

"I know some. I been going to church all my life."

"Really?" I said.

"Yeah, after yesterday, you wouldn't think so, would you? I don't know why I acted the way I did. I'm embarrassed."

"That's all right. I'm glad we're friends now. Cameron too. I think you did us a favor, to tell the truth."

"How's that?"

"Dad bought some deodorant."

"You mean you didn't have any?"

"Didn't know what it was."

Jason watched out the window a minute, cows and horses and trees, men working their fields. "How do you know the sheriff?"

The thought crossed my mind that he didn't need to know, but why not. "He picked us up on the road last night, after church."

"You didn't have a ride?"

"Dad said he would come, but he didn't. We were 'bout to our lane when the sheriff drove up."

The bus bounced once then ground to a stop, its brakes as grating as fingernails on a chalkboard.

Jason looked over my shoulder, across the intersection. "That's him! That's the motorcycle I saw last night."

The three of us stuck our noses to the window. "I thought you didn't pay attention to it," Cameron said.

"The white star on the side of his helmet. I saw it last night."

29

Cindy wasn't on the bus and didn't come to school. I hoped she wasn't sick, or something bad had happened in her family.

The cowboy sat next to another girl in math class, filling her ear with his goings on. He just liked to talk, stir a pot, and he didn't care who with. I gave his stare my back to look at.

It was only the second day of school, but it felt like summer break never happened, the same old thing all over again. The teachers and kids were all the same. A few new faces walked the halls, but not many. Maybe high school would be different. Long as they served a lunch and we didn't have to rely on Momma Ray for table scraps, or Dad for money, I wouldn't care.

I set my mind to my schoolwork. The day passed in a flash, with a short intermission to inhale roast beef and mashed potatoes with gravy and a chocolate chip cookie. When I took my tray to the trash, someone had left a cookie. I snatched it up and put it in a napkin. Cameron would appreciate sharing half of it after chores.

When the bus door opened, I walked out and lit a shuck for the house. Jake fell in beside me. He was being his usual self, tail going crazy. A quick scruff on the head didn't satisfy him, but it would have to do for now.

"Hey, wait." Cameron waved bye to Jason over his

shoulder. "What's your big hurry?"

"Mr. Bryan assigned a chapter in the science book and Miss Betty Sue gave us a page of math problems. I want to get on with it before Dad comes up with something for us to do."

"I don't like math much. Some of that geometry stuff doesn't make sense to me. Proving a line's straight is simple. Get a ruler. All them shapes and symbols. How do folks learn that stuff? I didn't see nothing in the book shaped like a hog trough. I might understand something like that."

"I don't know, but whatever. I'm not getting behind on my schoolwork this year. Somehow, I'm going to get it all done."

Cameron skipped twice, first one knee then the other raised high. "Sure you are. So am I. We're dumb, remember? Dad said so. Wait, I know. Next time he blows a cork over our grades, we can ask him to hit us with our books, or better yet, tape our homework to his foot. When he kicks us, we might absorb some knowledge through our hind ends."

I gave Cameron my that's-not-funny look. He only smiled and continued. "Long as the hayfield and chores mean more to Dad and Momma Ray than our school work, we're going to struggle with our grades. It's not our fault, it's theirs."

Cameron was right. Today, if the house was empty, both of them gone, I'd have time for homework. Otherwise, there was no telling what was in store for us.

"Ty, wait up. What are we going to do with the motorcycle guy?"

"What's there to do?"

"What if he's making shine back in the woods? Or

there's a jail escapee, a bandit hiding back there. Bet he's got a bunch of money hidden. Reckon it's that old shack back of the holler where Jake lost his eye?"

"You fell off your rocker. It takes wood and fire to make shine."

"Well, Ty, everyone knows that." Cameron's voice went shrill, like Momma Ray talking.

"Well, Cameron," I responded no less sarcastic. "Have you seen anyone hauling wood, heard a chainsaw running, or smelled smoke? And if someone's hiding, why does he leave? That ain't hiding, that's coming and going. And you think I've got an imagination."

Cameron caught up and fell in step next to Jake. "Heck, I don't know. Maybe he likes to eat at The Burger Stop every night."

Jake trotted in front of us and put his nose to the ground, working the scent where the biker turned off, then left a piddle on a bush.

Jake's actions got me to wondering again, pondering why and where he did what he did. Dogs were sure strange sometimes.

Cameron walked a few paces into the brush, crouched, and then pulled a blade of grass and put it between his teeth. "You going to help me set a trap? We'll find out who's been coming down here and why."

"Just what kind of trap you got in mind?"

"I've been thinking about that." Cameron held his hands out flat, palms down, and waved them over the area. Looked like he could already see his plan in action. "We could take some of them boards we pulled off that old barn to build the chicken house we never finished. We lay them out right through here and cover

161

them with leaves. There's plenty of nails in them. He'll get a flat."

"Yeah, or step on one and get hurt. We can't do that."

Cameron stood and looked around. "Maybe a bunch of cans tied together and strung right across here on some baling twine would work. Then, we lie in wait and catch him."

I was done with Cameron's wild ideas. He wasn't listening. "We'll hear him coming on the motorcycle, won't need no cans. And catch him? You going to tie him up, or jump on him and chew on his ear 'til he cries uncle?"

Cameron gave a quick snort, jerked the blade of grass out of his mouth, and started for the house. "You ain't right. Now you're the one who's no fun, ruining the moment. I have a good plan. It'd be something to do. You don't want to help me, just say so, and I'll do it myself. Or don't say so. Up to you."

"You're running on. I've got homework to do, and I'm going to read some Bible verses 'fore Dad lines us out, if he ain't already got plans."

"Well, you just get to gnawing on it. I don't have any. I'm going to get some of them old boards and cans ready."

"How is it you don't have homework? You have Miss Betty Sue after me."

"I did it during health class. I hate homework and you know it."

Focusing was my problem, or daydreaming was. If I'd concentrate, there was no reason for me not to have my homework finished before leaving school. "Cameron, let's just go down the road and sit a spell tonight. If the motorcycle comes, we'll ask him what he's doing."

"I'll think on it. Look, we're in luck. Dad's pickup's gone and the doors are closed. Momma Ray went with him."

Jake plopped down in the shade of a bush with his tongue hanging out.

Setting a trap for the motorcycle rider would be something to do. It had a feel of excitement to it. Someone had been in the woods and that was a fact. It would be fun to find out who and why.

Momma Ray preferred we study in our room, sitting on our bed with a book for a desk, but she wasn't home. I sat and placed three books on the kitchen table, the science book, the math book and the red book, the New Testament. It took some doing, I wanted to pick up the red one, but math had to come first.

Evening found me in the red book, reading words printed in red. Cameron had been right about "thee" and "thou," and I'd have to add "hath" and "doeth" to the list. Some of it was hard to understand. Jesus seemed to be a good guy, someone to know, someone to rely on. Jason had more questions he'd need to answer for me.

Shadows were long when I walked out. There was still no sign of Dad and Momma Ray. Jake had wandered off. Probably with Cameron.

The four tomatoes I found on the ground in the garden wouldn't be missed. Two of them went down on the spot. The other two I carried down the road where Cameron worked on setting his trap.

"About time you showed up."

I held out the tomatoes. "You want these? Sorry, I'm a slow reader, you know."

"Yeah, I'm hungry. Where'd you find them?" Cameron tried to give one back to me.

"On the ground in the garden. That's yours. I ate my two. I wonder where Dad's at? It'll be dark soon."

"Who cares? It's peaceful." Cameron took a bite and sucked juice as it dripped, and then he wiped his chin. "Don't walk over there. I got boards covered in leaves. And right through here," he swallowed and pointed with the tomato, "is a string of tin cans."

"Looks like you got it all covered."

"Let's move into the woods a ways and sit for a spell."

"And when Dad comes home?"

"Skedaddle through the woods for the barn. We're finishing up chores. He'll never know."

We found a spot where we could relax. Jake laid his head on my lap and sniffed at the cookie in my shirt pocket. Might as well break it in half and enjoy it.

Cameron leaned against a tree and stretched out his legs. "Did you read the Bible?"

"I did. You're right about some of the words, kind of confusing. Here, I saved this from lunch."

"Oh, T, thanks."

Jake sat up in front of me. "No begging. Lay down."

"Wait, listen. What's that noise? Dad?"

I turned my head. Jake pushed away from me and disappeared into the darkness. "That's not Dad. It's a motorcycle."

We scrambled to our feet and moved to the edge of the road. The motorcycle came toward us, slow and dark, its engine a deep hum, not loud like a racing bike. The engine died, but the bike kept coming, coasting, the gravel noisy under its tires. It stopped and brush rustled. There were other noises I couldn't identify: metal on metal, clicking, someone taking a deep breath.

Something Cameron didn't figure on was the guy riding the bike would have to see to park in the same place every time. He missed the trap by a good twenty paces.

My heart beat like a bass drum.

Cameron whispered. "Let's get closer."

I put a hand on his shoulder and we inched forward through the brush, one branch, one carefully placed foot at a time. "Where's Jake?" I whispered. "Why don't he cut loose?"

"I don't know. Maybe he went to the house. Listen. What's that?"

Crunching, like someone chewing. How far away I couldn't tell, twenty paces, thirty at the most. Then it dawned on me. "That's Jake eating something, a dog biscuit. The guy's made friends with Jake. That's why he ain't howling."

"Uh-oh, Dad's coming. Go to the barn. I'll be right back."

My hand fell on nothing. "Cameron, Cameron."

I lit out for the barn just as headlights appeared. Cameron was nowhere in sight. We were in a heap of trouble. Jake met me as I made it to the back door of the barn. He and I were going to have us another visit about taking food from a stranger. Dad rattled into the yard about the time I clicked on the light in the barn. He got out and walked toward me. "What you doing in there in the dark?"

My mind raced straight into a big fat lie. "The lights just came back on, Dad. They been off for a while."

His eyes narrowed. He had to think on that one. "Where's Cameron? You boys got chores done?"

"I…Cameron is…"

"I'm right here. Just back there with the pigs."

Cameron walking up from behind scared the daylights out of me. How he got there so fast was a miracle.

Dad and Momma Ray walked to the house.

Momma Ray stopped at the door. "Hurry up with chores. I'll make you something for dinner."

"Yes, ma'am." I turned to face Cameron. "Where'd you go? I was scared to death that guy got you."

"Nah, he didn't get me. I didn't see him, but he ran just like we did. I heard him stumble and fall. He went down hard or hit something and let out a big puff of air, sounded like Dolly coughing. He's riding a Yamaha motorcycle. It was hid off in the bushes about forty paces down the road."

"How do you know that?"

"I stole his helmet."

30

Boy, were things getting crazy, or what?

I tried to turn over and cover my head with the pillow, but I couldn't. I stared at the window. A branch on the bushes outside would move and my mind put a face on it.

"Cameron, you awake?"

"I am now."

"I can't sleep."

"So you don't want me to sleep neither?"

"Come on, Cameron. Think about it. Someone's been watching us. Gives me the creeps. How can you sleep?"

"I knew you'd keep watch."

"You did?"

"Of course not, but you're the worrier. Leave it be. Jake's out there."

I looked at the window again. I knew my dog lay there under the bush, as always. "He's a traitor. Done made friends with that guy, whoever he is. Jake might let him walk right up to the window."

"That's true, looks like he made a friend, but don't blame him. Dogs like a good biscuit." Cameron stirred, shaking the bed. "Guess what? Two things."

"Not playing."

"I wasn't trying to play."

"What, then?"

"No one wants to kidnap two hillbilly kids."

"I know that. What else?"

"The helmet is dark blue or black and has a white star on each side of it."

"Just like Jason said."

"Yep, but nothing else. No name, nothing."

"Cameron, you shouldn't have stole it." Here I was feeling guilty for something I didn't do.

"It'll make him think about coming back. He knows we're onto him now."

"He knew that when we took off running."

"Nah, Dad's pickup would cover a herd of cattle running, and I didn't run until I hit the road. My chest almost popped before I got to the barn. I haven't run that hard in awhile."

"This is a strange deal, Cameron."

"Sure is. Why don't you be quiet and go to sleep? Morning's coming." Cameron was done. He turned over and tried to get my share of the covers.

Sleep felt far away…but it came…as did morning, and much too soon. Our rooster mouthed off outside the window, and I came wide-eyed like I'd been up an hour already. Sometimes I wished he'd find his way into Momma Ray's cook pot.

Jake's ears flapped. Hogs squealed and a ruckus erupted, but didn't last long. A light breeze passed by the sty before it reached the house. Oh, the smell of hogs. Nothing like it first thing in the morning.

Heavy footsteps came down the hall. Dad opened the door and screamed, "Hey!"

Cameron barely stirred.

"I'm awake, Dad." I sat up.

The light came on.

"You boys get up. I'm going to town this morning. Old man Jordan's going to pick you up after school.

Don't get on the bus. He'll bring you home tonight. Work, work, don't mess up."

The door banged shut.

Cameron didn't move, but whispered, "Did I hear him right?"

"Sure did. We need to take our work gloves to school with us."

"That's what I'm talking about. Don't let me forget mine. Mr. Jordan wanted us to work this weekend too. We could make some good money. Got to squirrel some away without Dad finding out." Cameron got out of bed and dressed. "Want to see the motorcycle helmet?"

"Yeah, I do. Where'd you put it?"

"In the barn. Come on."

Jake fell in beside me and Cameron. He acted like nothing happened, wagging his tail and jumping around. I felt betrayed. How could he do it? I ignored him, but he didn't seem to care and kept pressing me to pet him, looking at me with his big, brown eye. He didn't even act like he felt guilty about what he'd done.

Cameron marched straight into the barn and rummaged in the sacks under the wooden bench. He stood, looked around, and dug again. "That's odd. I know I put it here, but it's gone. T, someone got it."

We walked out the back of the barn and stared off into the woods like we didn't have no more sense than a goat.

"Cameron, you stole his helmet, and he come and stole it back. Now who's wondering?"

"Man, who'd have thought? I hid it good too."

"Let's get chores done. I'm hungry. Then we can get out of here."

About halfway to the bus stop, Dad passed us. We

didn't wave and he didn't wave.

"Cameron, do you love Dad?"

After a quick wave at the floating dust the pickup stirred, Cameron looked at me like I'd kicked him in the shin. "Heck no. We done talked about this. I don't love him."

"I do."

"How could you love him? He hates us and treats us like animals."

"I don't like him."

"That don't make sense. You love him, but don't like him? You need to go see a doctor. You ain't right in the head."

"Maybe not. It's just the way I feel."

"I don't see the difference."

We all arrived at the bus stop at the same time—Jason, the bus, me, and Cameron. Cindy was there and she sat alone. Our eyes met, and she used hers to point to the empty spot next to her. She moved her backpack so I could sit.

"Good morning, Ty."

"Morning, Cindy." I put my books on my lap and stared straight ahead. My tongue froze about the time my mind went blank.

"Ty, did we have math homework?"

"What? Oh, Miss Betty Sue gave us a page of problems. I got them all done, but I don't know if I did them right."

"I could help you, if you want. Help you with your homework sometimes. We could do it during lunch and on the bus."

What a better way to spend time with Cindy. "I worried about you yesterday, 'cause you didn't come to school."

"One of my cousins is sick, and Mom wanted me to go with her to the hospital to see him. He got out yesterday."

"Oh, I'm sorry. What's it like? A hospital, I mean."

Cindy's red lips pooched out like maybe she was going to give me a quick peck on the cheek, but I misread her. "Ty, you don't get out much."

"No, I suppose I don't. I've never been to a doctor. Cameron either."

"You didn't go when your Dad hit you in the mouth?"

It was my turn to be surprised. "How'd you know about that?"

"Ty Ray, I'm not blind. Yours and Cameron's lips were swollen the first day of school. I'm not the only one who knows how your dad treats you."

Her comment made me check the tooth with my tongue. Cameron hadn't been messing with his tooth lately, so his might be OK too.

We didn't talk much after that. Like with Cameron, I felt comfortable in the silence between us. When I glanced at her, she glanced back and smiled. She had a scar on her right knee. She pulled her green skirt down to cover it and heat rose in my face. I didn't realize I'd been so obvious.

Miss Betty Sue went over our homework in class, and it was a good thing. I didn't get a one of them right and would have failed. I know when something is less than or greater than something else, but I had the signs mixed up. I wanted Cindy's help—just to be with her—but I also wanted to get something right on a test for once.

Cowboy walked by on the way to the pencil sharpener and mouthed off about driving a pickup.

The words rolled off my feelings like water off a pig's back. Christmas wasn't far off. I was going to look into how much a kite cost, buy him one, and present it to him in front of the class.

As the day wore on, thoughts of Mr. Jordan and working took over my mind. He mentioned he had a fence to mend. And he said we'd be able to practice our driving skills. A stop at The Burger Stop could be in the mix. I wanted to see Randy, see how he felt. The bell rang.

Cameron stood at the curb. "I told Miss Adams we wouldn't be on the bus."

"What'd she say?"

"Nothing, just 'See you Monday'."

"That was easy. This is the first time we haven't ridden the bus home."

"There's Mr. Jordan, behind the red pickup."

Mr. Jordan pulled to the curb in front of us. I reached for the door handle, but before I could open it, he got out.

"Hello, boys. I hope you're well today and don't have too much homework. Ty, you drive."

I was stumped. "Sir?"

"Get over here and drive Cameron and me down to the end of the road. Hurry up. Folks want to get in here and get their kids."

I ran around the pickup, hopped in behind the wheel, and put on my seatbelt. Cameron looked as wide-eyed as I felt. I was in the ninth grade! I don't know what Mr. Jordan was thinking.

I looked up, and there stood Cowboy and Cindy. My heart soared. Cindy wore the biggest grin I'd ever seen. Cowboy looked like he'd choked on a mouthful of crow.

Cindy gave me a quick wave.
I put her in gear and eased out the clutch.

31

I drove to the main road, pulled to the side, and stopped. Mr. Jordan hopped out and I slid over. My cheeks hurt. I couldn't remember smiling that much, not in all my days.

Mr. Jordan and Cameron had matching grins. "Ty, you did well, son. Well, I tell you. Cameron, when we get to the house, you can take a turn."

"Yes, sir. I appreciate the lesson."

"You boys hungry? Did you get enough for lunch today? We can stop and get you something if you didn't."

Me and Cameron looked at one another. Stopping to get something to eat would be wonderful, but we'd had plenty—at least I know I did. Today was chilidog and fries day, and I'd managed to find two extra dogs to eat.

"No, sir," I said. "We had a good lunch. We're ready to go."

"I don't think I'm going to work with you today. Randy has been sick, sicker than normal. We had to put him in the hospital right after you saw him, and he just got home. You remember Ed? He drove when we picked up hay. He's going to work with you at a place I'm leasing across from the house. The fences are a mess and wouldn't hold a cow any time at all." We pulled in, parked, and got out. "You men remember to bring your gloves?"

"Yes, sir, got them right here." I held up mine. I'm glad we remembered. They were like a gift.

Mr. Jordan pointed toward the barn. "I think Ed's getting supplies loaded in the ranch truck. See if you can give him a hand."

"Sir, would you tell Randy…tell him I'll say a prayer for him. I hope he gets well real soon."

Mr. Jordan looked at me, his blue eyes intense. The silence was long enough to make me fidget and poke at the grass with a toe. "I sure will, Ty. Thank you for that."

Praying wasn't something I'd ever done on purpose. Dad had forced me to request God's help a few times, and I didn't know if that was considered a prayer. Until we went to the white church, asking God for other things had never crossed my mind.

Ed had an armload of steel fence posts. He tossed them into the bed of an old, tan pickup, next to a roll of barbed wire, shovels, hammers and the like. He pulled the glove off his right hand and offered it. "Gentlemen, good to see you again. You ready?"

"Yes, sir," we said at the same time. We shook his calloused hand.

"Did you bring some work clothes?" He paused a moment as me and Cameron looked each other up and down. "No? I'll tell you what. I think there's a couple of shirts hanging in the tack room that Randy wears when he's doing chores. Let's see if they fit. I bet they do."

I put on a white cotton shirt. It had stains on it and a pocket was missing. The material was whiter where the pocket had been. Cameron put on a brown one. We hung our shirts where we got the replacements.

Ed eyed us. "That'll do. No use ruining a good

shirt. If we had some extra britches, I'd let you have them too, but we don't. OK, I think I've got everything we need in the pickup. Who wants to drive?"

I answered by walking around to the passenger's side.

Ed crawled in behind me and closed the door. "Well, men, the only thing wrong with manual labor is Manuel doesn't ever show up." He laughed and looked at me, then Cameron. "You don't get it?"

"I don't get what?"

He laughed again only louder. "Never mind. Cameron, this old truck is automatic, just put it in D for go. And remember that R don't mean race. Take a right at the end of the lane and a left at the first gate. It's open. Just drive in and stop."

Cameron looked at me and grinned.

Ed was going to be fun to work with.

The fence looked to be a mess, both wire and posts missing and broken. The wire that remained sagged.

Ed jumped out and opened the tailgate. "Let's start by replacing the bad posts along the road. Cameron, you and I will take the step-jack and that short piece of chain there and pull the bad posts. Ty, you bring the post pounder and a couple of posts at a time and put in a new one behind us. Have you driven posts before?"

"No, sir, not yet."

"Well, it's easy. Stand up the post, like so." He grabbed a steel post and held it with his left hand. "Then, put the post driver over the top of it and beat the dickens out of it. But stop before it reaches China."

We laughed at that one.

Ed continued. "Just make sure the notches are facing the same way. That's what supports the wire.

And keep them straight as possible. They bend easy enough, so if one is crooked, you can push it straight. You ready?"

Ed removed four strands of wire from the first post. Then he and Cameron tied a short piece of chain around the bottom of it, made a loop for the jack to fit in, and jacked it out of the ground.

Ed tossed the old post aside. "We'll drive by before we quit and pick these up. Cameron, carry the jack to the third post down, the bent one. Ty, come on and give her a try. Move it over 'bout a foot, so the post isn't in the same hole."

I placed the bottom of the post where I thought it should be, stepped back, so the post driver, which was only a piece of two-inch pipe—three feet long, with a piece of steel plate welded on top of it—could be slid over the top. It was heavy, about the weight of a half a sack of feed. After standing the two erect again, I gave it what for, and holy cow. My shoulders felt like they'd been set afire. After ten whacks, I couldn't do it anymore.

Ed laughed loud and long, and I joined him. Most of the time, when someone laughed at me, I'd take offense. But not this time. I must have looked a sight, and I enjoyed laughing at Ed laughing at me.

Cameron's mouth hung open as if he'd never seen the like.

Ed reached over and squeezed my left shoulder. "If this was a fight, the post just won, whupped you fair and square. Let the driver do the work. You just pick it up and help it start south. It'll do the rest. We have thirty or forty to replace, so don't kill yourself on the first one. You do four or five and Cameron can take a turn."

"Yes, sir."

He gave me a pat on the back. "You're just the right height for each post too. Drive them in until they're as tall as you are."

"Yes, sir."

He left me with it. I took another short rest after hitting it a few licks. Then I found my rhythm and started counting each stroke of the driver in my head. By the third post, I had my own competition going, trying to beat the number of strokes it took to drive the last post.

After five posts, Cameron had his turn. He must have taken a lesson from the beating I took because he looked like a pro.

The next thing I know, me and Cameron were following the pickup, throwing old posts in the back.

The sun was still high, a huge yellow ball sitting over the horizon, maybe an hour of daylight left. The evening would be cool and pleasant.

"Ty, it's funny." Cameron tossed in a post and walked to the next one.

"What's funny?"

"My arms are killing me and my hands are sore, but I feel wonderful."

"Me too. What is that?"

"I know what it is, but I don't know if I can say what I'm thinking." We walked to the next post together, quiet, while he looked for the words. "Fear. We work hard for Dad 'cause we're scared. I'm not scared here, and I work harder and I like it. I like it a lot."

Cameron amazed me sometimes. He was a thinker.

Ed stopped and we crawled in the cab with him

for the ride back to the barn. He pulled around to the side and backed up to a stack of old posts and wire. "Take the old posts out, if you would. I'm going to mosey up to the house and check in with the boss. I'll be right back and take you home. I've got a place we might stop too, if you're not in too big a hurry."

"We got no place to go." Cameron gave me a quick look and grinned.

I nodded my head. "My shoulders are going to be sore tomorrow."

"Mine too, but it feels good. What's next, I wonder?"

"I hope it's a burger, fries, and apple pie with a big soda pop to wash it down with."

"Yeah, that would top it off. Hey, look who's here."

I turned and suddenly felt like crawling under the pile of posts.

"Hi, Ty."

"Hi, Cindy."

32

Ed turned off of the main road before I got a glimpse of the sign above The Burger Stop. It was just as well. Seeing it would've made me hungry. Cameron kept staring at me like I had something stuck in my teeth. I raised my chin at him. "What?"

He whispered, "You're a moron."

I gave him my shut-up face. Cameron knew the face but didn't care. "You, brother, are a moron."

Cameron might get a kite the same day I give one to Cowboy if he didn't watch it. They can go fly them together. I shrugged him off and looked at houses and trees as we passed, like I didn't care what he said.

We weaved through town until I didn't have a clue where we were. Usually, I'd ask, but today I didn't give two hoots.

Ed slowed, flipped on the blinker, and then turned onto a dirt lot. The sign at the entrance, *The Coon Club*, hung on chains between two wooden posts.

Cameron leaned into me. "You ever heard of this place?"

He was trying to be nice, but I was still thinking about his "moron" comment. "Nope."

Ed parked among two-dozen pickups. "Come on, men. Let's go watch."

"What is it?" I asked.

"It's a swimming contest for coon dogs. You boys ever seen one before?"

Me and Jake

Cameron shut the door. "No sir, not yet."

The pond might have been fifty paces long and ten wide. To one side of the pond stood a small set of bleachers that would seat a dozen or so people.

Everyone seemed to know Ed because hellos and handshakes went around amid bays and barks of a dozen coon dogs. Black and Tans, Redbones, Beagles, and Walkers pulled at their leashes. A ruckus erupted when a Walker got loose and got into a fight with a Redbone.

An older man in a green ball cap walked up to Ed. He pointed at me and Cameron with his cigar as they talked. Ed looked our way, nodded, and then walked over. "They need someone to run the dog boxes and pedal the coon. You mind helping?"

"We'll help. What do we have to do?" I turned to look at my brother. "Eh, Cameron?"

"Yep, I'm in."

Ed led us to the other end of the pond where a set of four wooden dog boxes stood, side by side, like a starting gate. All the doors were linked together, so they'd open at the same time. Bolted to the top of the boxes was an upside-down bicycle with no front tire. The back tire had been replaced with a small wire cable that ran to a pulley on a tree across the pond and back—a continuous loop. A small cage hung by the wire and inside the cage was a wily bandit.

I pointed at the coon. "Cameron, I ain't seen one of those since you opened the door to our cage and got all scratched up and ate on."

He stuck out his tongue at me. "You're still a moron."

I puffed up as best I could. "Why do you keep saying that?"

"Cindy, she's Randy's cousin, Mr. Jordan's niece. She told him what Hillman said. They set you up."

"Well, I didn't know. You thought it was a coincidence too. She just told Mr. Jordan what Hillman said. It was Mr. Jordan's idea to let me drive."

Cameron's nose wrinkled. "Moron, moron."

Ed bent to inspect the boxes. "They're going to have four races today. Got twelve dogs, so four will swim in the first three races. The three winners will swim in the last one to determine the champion.

"Ty, why don't you run the boxes? The boys will load their own dogs, so you don't risk getting bit. They have a starting pistol. It shoots blanks. When it goes off, just pull the rope. All the doors will open at the same time. Cameron, you get to ferry the coon. Give it a try."

Cameron grabbed the bike pedals with both hands and gave them a whirl. The cage and its captive sped across the pond a couple of feet above the water's surface.

Ed put a hand on Cameron's shoulder. "That's good, but not so fast. You want to keep the cage just out of their reach. They've rigged the bike so it pedals both ways. Bring the coon back to the edge of the water. That should be a good starting point for you. This won't take long, and we'll go get a bite to eat before I take you home."

Oh, yeah. Me and Cameron slapped hands.

Cameron looked like a three-year-old sitting in front of a pile of honey-soaked pancakes. "Boy, Ty. Too bad ole Jake ain't here to run this. I bet he'd do good."

"I bet he would too."

The first four dogs to race were Jake look-alikes, and boy, did they have a set of lungs. The baying and howling the likes I never heard before. I'd have been proud to count any of them as my friend.

We got them in the boxes. Cameron eased the cage back, and they got wind of the coon. They bayed together, like they knew the same song.

Men lined the pond, but most sat in the bleachers at the finish line. They visited and smoked cigars and cigarettes, or chewed tobacco.

"You ready, boys?" came a yell from the finish line.

I raised a hand and yelled back, "Yes, sir!"

The gun popped, I jerked the rope, and the dogs came out of the boxes like a shot.

Cameron almost didn't get started fast enough, but managed to keep the coon just out of their reach all the way across.

Cheers rose as the first dog emerged from the pond, put his paws against the tree, bowed his back, and cut loose with a bay at the cage swinging above him.

Cameron could have been one of them big plastic dolls with a grin painted on its face, all his teeth showing. "Who won, Ty? Did you see?"

"A Black and Tan," I said.

"Well, duh. They were all Blacks."

We laughed.

Their owners scrambled to leash their dogs before one of them started a fight.

The next group consisted of a Beagle, a Redbone, and two Walkers. Beagles don't have much for legs and I wouldn't have given two hoots for this one's chances, but he nearly won. He came out of the water right on the heels of one of the Walkers.

A beautiful female Redbone won the third race.

She out-swam two Walkers and a Beagle by five paces.

Cameron cranked the cage back. "I wish I had a dollar."

"What for?"

"I'd bet on that little Redbone to win. She swims like a fish."

"A dollar to bet? I'd just like to have a dollar. That would buy two little cheeseburgers. I'd bet, but not for money."

"That don't make sense. Bet just to bet?"

"Yeah, it does. You're either right or wrong, but don't lose nothing."

Cameron waved me off. "Here they come with the winners. I bet you the Redbone wins."

I opened the back of the boxes, so they could load the dogs. "I bet she wins too."

Cameron's Scrooge look appeared. "I picked her first. You got to pick another one."

"All right. I'll take the Black and Tan. That Walker's too skinny. He floats like I do. He'll be lucky if he makes it across a second time."

The gun popped and I pulled the rope. All three dogs swam neck and neck. It would be close.

A hat flew in the air, then glasses, and someone yelled. Out of the bleachers hopped a white-haired man with a cigar in his mouth. Then he dove in the pond, clothes, cigar and all. "Cameron, look. A man's gone crazy. Jumped in the pond like he don't got no sense. Ha! There goes three more in after him."

Cameron watched and pedaled at the same time, shaking his head at the sight.

About the time the Redbone came out of the water to win the contest, the old man who had jumped in crawled out, dragging the Walker.

"I told you, Cameron. I knew that Walker wasn't going to make it. Like to drowned. The old feller had to jump in and save his dog."

Cameron pulled the coon back. We slapped hands again. What a hoot.

Ed trotted toward us. "Good job, men. Let's get out of here. You hungry?"

Me and Cameron hopped down and joined him.

Cameron indicated his charge. "What about the coon?"

"One of the guys will take care of him. They'll feed and water him. He's well taken care of."

Just over Ed's shoulder I caught a glimpse of a blue pickup that looked too familiar. My heart bounced off the roof of my mouth.

33

The bare bulb above the barn door cast just enough light to enhance shadows and make them darker. Every nook and cranny looked like a bottomless pit that could hold an untold number of spiders and mice.

Cameron sat on a sack of chicken feed. I'd turned over an old wooden box. Jake sat next to me watching my hand as it moved back and forth from my mouth to the box of French fries. I slipped him a bite of meat. He swallowed and licked his chops.

"Cameron, look at Jake. He's smiling."

"No, he's not."

"Look at him. You ain't looking. He is too. His teeth are showing."

"He licked his mouth and his lips got caught in his teeth. That ain't a smile."

Cameron reached for his drink and took a big noisy sip. "You scared me to death when you said you saw Dad. That pickup sure looked like his—beat up, rusted and all. The man driving wasn't fat enough. I knew it wasn't Dad right off."

"No, you didn't."

"Did too." He shook out another French fry and crunched it. "And you're still a moron." He leaned toward me, like I wasn't paying attention. "And dogs can't smile."

Cameron leaned back, stretched out his legs and

crossed one foot over the other. "I will say this. Mr. Jordan sure made ole Cowboy eat crow. I'll never forget the look on his face."

"Yeah, we'll see what kind of looks he gives me Monday on the bus."

The last bite of burger sat on a dozen fries. My apple pie tucked away in my shirt pocket would taste good just before bedtime.

It wasn't like I planned to make Cameron covet the last of my dinner, but I knew it wouldn't be but a minute and he'd have his eyes glued in my direction. Saving some, forcing myself to wait, had a measure of satisfaction he'd never understand.

Cameron cleared his throat and sucked at his straw. "I sure enjoyed the dog swimming contest. Who thinks of stuff like that?"

"I don't know, but you're right. It was fun to watch."

"Dad and Momma Ray sure been spending a lot of time on the town or wherever they go. Kind of peaceful lately."

"Yep, sure is, ain't it? Ed sure is a hoot to work with. Got all them sayings and stuff. He's a worker too." I picked up the bite of cheeseburger and bit it in half.

"Yeah, and he don't yell—him or Mr. Jordan either one." Cameron let out a good puff of air. "Would you just eat that already? You nibble at your food like a girl."

"I don't either."

"Yes, you do. Just like Momma Ray even. Like you only got a couple of teeth and they're top and bottom, but not across from each other. I'm going to quit sitting with you. It's enough to drive me crazy, watching you pick at your food. I bet ants carried off a French fry and you didn't even know it, you eat so slow. Might as well give it to me."

OK, maybe I did take my sweet time to razz him. He sure could run on about it.

Light crossed the doorway. The rattle of Dad's pickup pulling into the yard followed it. We scrambled to hide the bags and wrappers. Jake took his leave out the back.

One pickup door slammed, then the other. Gravel crunched under heavy, rapid feet. The doorway filled with Dad's frame. "What are you boys doing in here? Got your chores done?"

Cameron moved a step away from me, his gaze focused to my left. I gave the top of the workbench a quick glance. Dear, Lord, I'd left my drink there.

"No, sir," I said. "We haven't done our chores yet. We, we just got home. Ed brought us. Randy Jordan's sick and Mr. Jordan couldn't."

"You didn't just get home. Don't lie to me. It's a mile to the county road, and we ain't passed a car for five miles."

"Well, we were talking, that's all," Cameron added.

"Where's my money?"

Cameron laughed.

Dad didn't even react to it. Just kind of turned his head Cameron's direction, worked the chaw in his mouth, and stuck out his chest. "You think something's funny?" He spit. The slime landed at Cameron's feet.

Cameron looked like he grew an inch taller just before he spoke. "We did all the work. How is it *your* money?"

Oh, he shouldn't ought to have said that. The color

in Dad's face rose to a boiling point.

I broke in. "We didn't get paid. Ed said Mr. Jordan would take care of it Sunday afternoon, after work."

Dad's stare moved back to me. His eyes met mine and moved down to my shirt pocket. I remembered the apple pie.

"Where'd you get that?"

I knew what he was talking about, no need to pretend or play dumb. "Ed bought it for me."

Then he saw my drink and howled like a coon caught in a trap.

Cameron stepped between me and Dad just as his big right hand left his side, aiming for my head. Cameron took the blow on the shoulder, but he stood his ground.

Then, from out of nowhere it seemed, Dad produced the broken shovel handle I'd used to hold off his old sow. I must have leaned it next to the door. It struck Cameron on the head with a big crack and dropped him like he'd been shot.

Blood splattered, and Cameron fell limp as a dead rabbit. Something screamed at me to run, but I couldn't. Dad had his eye on me, and still I stood there. Dad didn't give Cameron so much as a glance, just stepped over him like he would a run-over squirrel on a dirt road.

A scream escaped my lungs without me telling it to, and I sprang for the door. Dad moved quicker than a fat man should, but missed me with his big right hand.

After being in the light of the barn, I couldn't see a thing. The old yellow washing machine stood right in front of me, the boards for the hen house and the house frame just beyond that. I veered left then cut back right, headed for the woods like the boogieman was on my tail. His breath came in gasps, labored and loud, right on my heels.

From my right, Jake growled and the biggest ruckus I ever heard erupted behind me. Dad went down hard. Air exploded from his lungs. Jake snarled and his teeth snapped. Dad yelped. Jake must have taken a bite. A dull thud sounded, then Jake yelped. Dad got him one with the shovel handle for sure.

Somewhere I found a second wind and hit the timber on the run. Jake passed me on my left and took the lead. My eyes adjusted enough for me to see tree trunks and avoid them, but limbs and leaves slapped and grabbed at my face and clothes. A scream behind made me run harder, the blood rushing in my ears like radio static pulsing to the beat of my churning legs.

We slowed and my wind came back. The land rolled up and down. Rocky slopes, hardwoods, and brush-choked hollers passed as Jake led me on.

The holler where Jake lost his eye lay off to my left, but that wouldn't do because Dad knew about the old shack back there. And if Cameron had been right about the motorcycle guy, he might be hiding in it.

Oh, Cameron. He had to be dead. My knees burned, scraped from falling. Jake leaned against me. I cried on his neck. My tears like hot coals rolling down my cheeks. My chest squeezed the air from my lungs, so I had no breath to make sound.

The flood ran dry and we sat, Jake to my right, looking at me. "Oh, Jake, I should have killed Dad when I had the chance. Just dumped him out of the boat and drowned him. It would have been easy. But I didn't, too worried about my own feelings and what God would think. Now, I've killed my brother and friend. It's my fault."

Jake rose and walked several feet. He looked back at me and took another step. If dogs could talk he would have said, "Follow me, Ty Ray."

My legs felt heavy as my heart.

Jake took me deeper into the woods, into the dark of night at an easy pace, but before long, sweat washed the tears from my cheeks.

After a time, the smell of mildew drifted across my nose and the air cooled. The damp smell reminded me of our clothes after we washed them in the sink and hung them in our room to dry. The sound of water gurgling came from just in front of me. I caught the shimmer of light off the water.

"Thanks, Jake. You are an angel."

After drinking our fill, Jake padded over to a big oak tree—its old leaves noisy under his feet—turned a couple of circles, and plopped down.

I sat next to him and he put his head on my lap. My teeth chattered as if something had control of them and set them off without telling me. Cold crept up my back.

Jake didn't care when I curled up next to him.

My eyes opened, my mind alert. Jake stood a few feet away, looking back the way we'd come.

I jumped and ran, didn't even wait to see what he saw or smelled.

34

Jake caught me about the time my lungs screamed for air and brought me to a walk. A screech owl cut loose behind us. We both took a peek back.

Might have been a deer or a skunk, even a mountain lion, but taking a chance on Dad finding me would have been foolish. Jake's boar hairs weren't standing on end for nothing.

The woods turned a light gray as dawn crept through the trees, revealing hollers choked with brush. Before long the leaves would turn into a rainbow of colors. I made for the ridgeline to my right, topped out, and set a direction for the lighter part of the sky, due east.

Jake turned left.

"Jake, why do you want to go that way? Too hard to walk in a holler, the brush is thick. Stay out of there." My voice sounded strange and loud. A quick look confirmed that besides bugs, birds and maybe a critter I couldn't see, no one heard me talking to my dog.

Jake looked at me, and then walked another step north.

"Hey, this way. I don't want to cross another holler. You're not listening." I pointed east.

He ambled down the hill like my opinion was of no value.

"Jake, Jake, wait!" On second thought, east didn't

mean a thing, though town was east, six, seven miles distant. Maybe sunlight drew me that direction.

Walking in the holler wasn't bad. The slope was gradual, the ground was firm, and the brush was thin. Another little creek crossed our path. Jake would bail off in the water most times, but we followed it until we found a dead tree across a narrow part. The water might have been two feet deep at the most, but walking in soggy shoes had no appeal.

We drank together and moved on.

My new brown shirt had a big tear in the front. A red, sore streak crossed from my bellybutton to my right hipbone. Hadn't even noticed when it happened or what might have caused it. No telling what I ran through escaping that maniac.

All it took to set him off was the sight of a soda cup. A lit stick of dynamite was more predictable. Cameron's comment about money hadn't helped, but Dad always had something in his craw about what we ate and drank, like he was jealous. I remembered the apple pie then and felt my pocket, but it was gone. The ants would be having a feast when they found that this morning.

Thoughts of Cameron caused my heart to ache and tears to form again. I stumbled, stopped and wiped my eyes.

Good thing I had on my old shoes.

"Jake, wait. Where we going? We're just walking. We need a plan. We got to find someone and tell them about Cameron." I crawled over a log. "Don't look back at me like I'm dumb and keep walking. Come." I raised my voice. "Jake, come."

He hesitated then walked to me and sat at my feet. "Sometimes you seem to forget I'm the boss. Why are we walking north? There ain't a thing up that way. Only hills to climb and I'm tired. No hills, you hear me? Come to think on it, I'm hungry."

Jake's ears were up and he cocked his head left then right as I talked. "If folks heard me talking to you they'd think I fell off my rocker. They'd send me off to the duck farm."

Looking around, I realized Jake was right again. We had to go somewhere other than the middle of nowhere. I tried to remember what lay to the north. Our hayfield was north and a little west, but nothing else came to mind.

"All right, let's keep going, bound to be something ahead of us. But I'm telling you, I ain't climbing no mountains."

We walked until forever, it seemed. Looking back looked the same as looking forward, trees and brush and more trees. A doe and her fawn spooked and ran up the ridge, their tails like white flags waving goodbye. Brush and limbs cracked as they broke from cover, but after their first leap, they never made another sound.

Jake stopped and watched them for a second, then walked on. He seemed to know I followed him, since he kept clear of fallen trees and places hard to pass through.

I watched my feet and the ground in front of me. Jake's rear end tracked left then right, like it wanted to go off on its own but couldn't.

Jake stopped. Trees thinned to our front. A big pasture, recently cut, with two long rows of square bales stacked three high to one side. No house in sight, so I stepped into the open and continued walking. The going was easy, the same as walking across a lawn.

Jake went by me like he did when a coon hopped from a tree branch and hit the ground running. A hundred paces away, a rabbit hopped for all he was worth. Jake probably had him in mind for breakfast. The pair disappeared over a rise. Jake gained ground with every stride. The rabbit's ears were pinned back, and he was giving him a good run.

Jake trotted back minutes later, tongue hanging.

"So, he bested you. Don't feel bad. He had a head start. You just ran out of pasture, didn't you?" He got a good scruff on the head. "I wouldn't help you eat a rabbit, Jake. It's got to be cooked 'fore I'll put it in my mouth, and I got no way to make a fire."

We hit another patch of woods and then a smaller clearing where a trailer house stood. I watched for a minute, circled it to one side, staying back in the trees. No cars and no activity. White sheets and a mix of colors in bath towels hung on a line behind the house. Just beyond that stood a small, blue, plastic swimming pool and a rusty swing set with one seat hanging crooked.

My gaze went from the house to the garden behind it. I'd never been a thief, unless stealing tomatoes out of our own garden counted, but my belly was about to start eating its way out and go find its own food if I didn't get something in there soon. They wouldn't miss a few tomatoes or an ear of sweet corn.

"Jake, gardening season's 'bout over, but maybe there's something left. Let's go look."

Jake followed me this time.

There weren't but four rows of corn, ten paces long each, and they'd been picked over already. I managed to find two small ears and tucked them in a pocket. Two tomatoes disappeared on the spot, and I took two more for later.

"Jake? Jake, where'd you go? Come." Jake trotted around the corner of the house with a bone. "Where'd you find that?" His tail wagged twice and we made our way back into the woods.

I found a tree stump to sit on and shucked the corn. "How's your bone, Jake? Worms been eating this corn I found. Wish I could boil it and put on some butter and salt. That would be the cat's meow."

Jake stretched out on his belly with his back legs behind him, holding the bone with his paws. His eye closed when he gnawed at it. Then it opened when he got a piece to turn loose. He paused, let the bone lay, and stood, head high, smelling the wind.

"It's a hundred paces to the house, relax."

A door slammed, a pickup door, and dogs barked. That's all we needed to hear. I was done eating. Jake too. We lit out east to clear the place and then turned north again.

"This is dumb. I could have talked to the people who live in the trailer. They got a kid, maybe two. Why else would they have a little pool? But maybe they got a big dog, huh Jake? One of those dogs sounded big."

We walked through another holler and over a ridge with no end in sight. Morning and afternoon, passed. Shadows grew in length by the minute.

The smell of wood smoke stopped me in my tracks. Then I got a whiff of something that really took me home: pigs. "Easy, Jake. Don't go too fast."

The little stone house had a couple of rooms at the most with a stone chimney to one side. Smoke hung over the small clearing like morning fog.

A short man, hunched at the shoulders, wearing jeans and a blue shirt walked out the back door with a red bucket. He whistled a tune I'd never heard. It was a good tune, a happy tune. About halfway to a low shed he stopped and looked our direction. His gaze covered the hundred paces between us and made me look away. The tune ended on a long, low note.

My heart hit four hard beats before he started walking again. The tune took up where it ended. He turned the bucket over and pigs squealed.

Could this man feel my stare? No way.

Watching him amble back into the house brought to mind Dad's comment about knowing the woods and warning us not to run away.

"Jake, I don't know. This feller might know Dad and call him. What do we do now?"

Jake stared at the house. The end of his nose pulsed as he sniffed the air. He made no effort to move. A couple of stars twinkled overhead. Too late to make a wish on one.

I know wishing didn't do any good, but if I'd known how to pray I might have tried that.

"Jake, night's coming fast. I don't know what to do anymore. I thought I could live in the woods forever— just you, me, and Cameron. But Cameron's gone. Who do I trust besides you and Cameron? I need to call Mr. Jordan."

We sat quiet for a spell.

"Jake, I don't see a garden. I'm hungry. We got to find something to eat. The cheek-lady said I don't have no meat on my bones. Soon there won't be no bones neither."

"Boy, don't you move. And my name ain't Jake."

Might as well been Dad standing behind me. Like to scared me back to yesterday. Don't move? I had to move. I didn't have boar hairs like Jake, but goose bumps jumped out all over me, like the cold skin on a plucked chicken. There was no sitting there. The man had sneaked up behind me, holding a big pistol in his right hand, a sweat-stained brown hat pulled low over his eyes. He worked a chaw and spit, but not in my direction.

"Sir," I said.

"No, you just be quiet. Let's me and you mosey down to the house."

"Sir, my dog. I got to get Jake."

"I don't see no dog. You got an imaginary dog you like to talk to? I heard you as I walked up. I got two Black and Tans penned at the house. They'd know if another dog got within half a mile of here. Start walking."

Jake must have disappeared while I talked about Cameron, not paying attention. Didn't even see him leave, and he didn't warn me someone was coming.

The man motioned with his chin. "Let's go."

I couldn't help it. I cried.

35

The hand that touched my shoulder belonged to a gun-toting stranger who thought he'd caught a thief or who knows what, but it stopped the tears. The blue eyes set in the weathered face below the dirty hat had a warm, understanding glow to them. The face seemed somewhat familiar, but from where? I was pretty sure we'd never met.

He squeezed my shoulder for a second, and then he turned loose. "What's your name, son?"

"Ty."

"Ty?" His eyes held mine, one gray eyebrow raised.

I didn't want to tell him, but I did. "Ray, Ty Ray."

He switched hands with the pistol and offered the right one. "Imagine that. Call me Ray-Ray."

We shook. "Ray-Ray?" I wiped my eyes with the sleeve of my shirt. "Did...did your momma stutter or something?"

He chuckled, low and steady, wiped a hand across the white stubble on his chin, and then laughed outright. "No, son, she didn't. But that's a good one. Never thought of it. I guess it's something a woman who doted on her son would call him when he was a baby. It stuck."

"I'm sorry. I didn't mean to be, be rude 'bout your name."

"That's OK. You weren't rude, just honest. Been

199

called worse. Let's mosey up to the house, you and me."

"My dog, Jake, he heard you coming and sneaked off without me. He's out there somewhere."

"So you did have a dog. I thought you were plum crazy when I walked up behind you and heard you talking. I don't get many visitors, especially arriving from the direction you came from. You can imagine my concern. Call your dog, see if he'll come."

I gave Jake a yell, then another, but nothing stirred.

Ray cleared his throat and motioned for me to follow. "Son, he'll come around. The smell of my old dogs might be keeping him away. Come on to the house. I need to finish chores before it gets dark. I don't have a flashlight and my old eyes don't see too good anymore at night. Then, we'll get a bite to eat and talk about life."

I wasn't in the mood to talk about anything, much less life. And whose life? Mine? It would be a short conversation. Food didn't even sound good.

Ray's boots had seen better days, run over on the outsides, heels worn down. A hitch in his get-a-long made him limp, the step with his right leg longer than the one with the left. He whistled the same tune.

Jake had to be back in the woods watching and wondering. But he didn't show himself. I scanned the edge of the clearing for signs of him.

Two Black and Tans, heavier than Jake, opened up as we neared the house. Three young pigs rooted around a wooden trough under the shed, held in by chicken wire strung between posts. A small garden fenced by two strands of barbed wire looked neat and clear of weeds. Two rows of corn had been picked bare. The stalks already pulled and piled to one side.

Ray opened the door, put the pistol just inside on the counter, and grabbed a tin pail. "You know how to squeeze a teat?"

"Yes, sir. We got an old cow, but she's been dry a spell."

"Here." He held the pail out for me. "Squeezing teats isn't something a feller forgets over time. My old cow's called Miss May. She's around the side of the house there, keeping the lawn trimmed, I imagine. See if she'll give you a bucket full. She's got manners and don't kick, so help yourself."

"Miss May? That's a doozie name for a cow."

"Well, it's not complicated. She may or may not let you milk her. Or that used to be the case, therefore the name. She's mellowed in her old age, like me. Get the milk and we'll have some vittles."

To me, a cow is a cow. Miss May, or may not, was the brown milking type with one stubby horn curled down over her right eye. Her udder hung full and swung like the pendulum in an old clock as she walked. She looked back with a big brown eye and stopped as I approached.

Most times you'd put a cow in the barn and tie her head to milk her, but Ray didn't mention what to do since he didn't have a barn. I knelt next to her, positioned the pail, and went to squeezing.

Milking gave me time to think. Run or stay? Dark woods lay only seconds away. Tell Mr. Ray about Cameron or keep quiet? Dad said he knew everyone for miles. Threatened to find us and take care of us. The meaning in that threat was not lost on me and Cameron.

For now, I'd be keeping my mouth shut. If Mr. Ray

had a bunch of questions, he might not get all the truth for answers.

A faint light glowed behind dingy curtains at the back of the house. A shadow crossed the window. I gave the door a rapid tap with a knuckle.

"Come in. No need to knock."

Warmth and the aroma of I-couldn't-tell-what hit me when the door opened.

"Place the milk next to the sink, son." He never looked my direction.

The same kind of tan stone that covered the outside of the house was used for the floor on the inside. Against the wall to the left sat a white gas stove and fridge, like Momma Ray's. Under the window, to the right, was a counter with oak cabinets and a sink. It, too, was white.

No sign of the pistol.

Ray stirred fixings in a cast iron pan on a potbelly stove across the room. Next to it stood a small, round oak table with two matching chairs.

He took a small log from a wooden box next to the stove, tossed it in and closed the door. "Ty, I live simple. You don't mind simple, do you?"

Simple? I knew simple. "No, sir, not at all."

"Good, I don't have running water. Got electricity, but don't use it except for the fridge only because I like my milk...and I hate warm milk. I pump my own water. When it's bath time, my arms get tired." A grin spread across his face, slow like. He waited a second for me to get it and I did, but the humor wasn't in me at the moment. "That's an oil lamp behind you, this one above me too, and as you can see, I cook on a wood-burning stove. Lamp oil is cheap and wood only costs a little sweat and time. I still got lots of sweat. Not much time, but lots of sweat.

"I got my plate, never put it up. Only wash it. Grab you one from the cabinet by the window. And a fork from the drawer below it. You won't need a knife. We're going to have a bite of stew so tender the toothless could eat with us. You like venison and taters?"

At the mention of it my belly did a jig, and my mouth watered like it did at the mention of Burger Monster. I nodded.

Ray tapped the wooden spoon against the side of the pan, dipped a bite, and sampled it with a noisy slurp. "Ooh, it's hot enough. Perfect. Bring your plate over and help yourself, there's plenty. I'll get us a cup of milk. You like it cold or fresh from the cow? As I mentioned, I like it cold."

"Cold's fine, thanks."

Ray wasn't much for cutting the carrots and taters into small pieces, but the stew had plenty of both and a good helping of meat, all mixed in a thick broth. I put a dip on my plate and put the ladle back in the pot.

"Ty, I don't eat much. Put yourself another helping or two on there. You look like you could eat a side of beef in one sittin'. Though it's not far, it'll save you a trip to the stove."

I sampled and chewed the first bite, minding my manners. It hit bottom and my manners left me. The spoon wasn't big enough.

When my cup ran dry, he refilled it and brought the stewpot to the table. "Son, I think you got a hole in one leg to store food in, like a camel does on his back."

"Yes, sir, I was pretty hungry."

"There's only a tad left." He ladled it onto my plate. "This enough or do I need to make another batch? You ate everything but the pot."

"I didn't mean to eat so much."

"Hey, a man's got to eat. Don't you worry about it. Lots of deer in the woods and taters in the ground."

He pushed back his chair, took a toothpick from a coffee cup on the table, and crossed one leg over the other. "Tell you what. I have a good-sized bone with plenty of meat still on it I've been saving for my dogs. I'll put it outside the door. If your Jake comes looking for something to eat, it'll be there for him."

"I appreciate that."

Our eyes met. Again, his held mine in easy silence.

Ray worked the toothpick, and then he stopped and uncrossed his legs like he'd made up his mind about something. "You look like you got a case of hog fever."

"Hog fever? Never heard of something like that."

"Yep, after a hog eats, he'll lay down beside the trough and take a nap every time."

Just to prove his point, my eyelids got too heavy to hold up, and I yawned.

"Your room is down the hall on the left. It's dark as the inside of a cow in there right now. If you need a light, I'll get you a lamp you can carry to bed with you."

"No, sir, Mr. Ray-Ray, I'll be fine. I'm not scared of the dark."

"I have to ask you a question before you retire for the night. What brought you so deep into the woods? There isn't a house three miles from here as the crow flies, near ten miles by road. If a man was hunting coons, he'd have him a shotgun, maybe a partner to share the hunt with."

"My dog led me here. I been following him since

last night."

"Ty, I'm a man who believes in minding his own business. I expect others to mind theirs, but I feel you're in need of help. You and your dog didn't strike out for parts unknown without a good reason."

My emotions threatened to surface again. Talking about my problems didn't happen on a good day, and then not with a stranger. This man could be one of Dad's friends. Beating around the bush or lying wasn't neighborly, and Ray had been more than. But I couldn't take the chance, not yet.

Ray's eyes never left my face, as if he could see my thoughts.

The kitchen counters didn't have a thing on them. No Little Piggy canisters arranged smallest to biggest, no jars of pasta or rice. The walls didn't have calendars, pictures or paintings, though a few square spots of off-colored white paint hinted that wall hangings had once occupied those spaces.

I needed to call someone, but who?

"Yes, sir," Ray said. "I like the simple life. Don't even have a telephone. I do have an old pickup that runs at times. Most times it don't."

Now how did he know what I looked for? "What if something happens? How do you call for help without a phone?"

"Son, I don't have anyone to call, except a brother. He checks on me from time to time."

This time I looked away. He'd see my heartache if I didn't.

"Son, you're not much of a talker. You don't know me, and you're wary. Caution will serve you well in the future. But I'm on your side. Tomorrow morning, after chores and breakfast, we'll see if we can get my old pickup to running on more than two cylinders. I'll take you anywhere you want to go, long as it ain't down to China. That sound all right?"

His eyes sparkled in the lamplight.

At that moment, I didn't care to go anywhere or do anything. My belly had all it could hold, and my eyelids grew heavier by the second.

Ray's dogs howled an eerie duet that announced an unwelcome guest.

"Jake! That has to be Jake." I bolted for the door.

36

My mind stirred, lost in unfamiliar quiet. No snore from Jake or steady breathing from Cameron. No pigs squealing. Sunshine lit my eyelids, but our old rooster had yet to open his big mouth. Not like Dad to leave us in bed after sunup either.

I opened my eyes and sat straight up in bed, a peach-colored bed in a peach-colored room. The ceiling and all four walls down to white baseboards were all peach. A white chest of drawers with thin gold patterns painted around the edges sat against the wall at the foot of the bed, a matching night stand, with a lamp—strawberries painted all over its base. On one corner of the dresser stood three ballerinas poised to dance in a circle around the shaft of a peach umbrella on the top of a peach music box.

A story mom read me and Cameron one day, long ago, came to mind. It had a Mad Hatter and teacups and all kinds of scary, talking animals. Alice would have a room like this one.

Then, I remembered being dead tired, going to bed in the dark, Cameron, Jake and the bay of Ray's hounds. I slipped from under the covers, jerked my britches on, and headed for the kitchen.

Ray looked up from a pan on the potbelly, spatula in hand. "Morning." My face must have told of my intent. "Ty, I'm sorry. There's no sign of Jake."

I walked to the door and put a hand on the knob.

"The bone we put out is still there. He hasn't been around, not that I've noticed."

It's not as though I didn't believe him, but I had to see for myself. He offered no further comment when I opened the door and stepped outside.

Yelling for Jake got a howl from Ray's dogs in return. Those two had a good set of lungs. Probably hear them tree a coon across two hollers and a ridgeline.

There was no sign of my friend.

Ray had traded the spatula for a fork and worked over the same pan. The door clicked shut behind me.

Jake had to come back, didn't he?

"Guess I overslept. What time is it?"

"It's morning time, after sunup and chores, but before lunch." He gave me a quick grin. "I own a watch, but haven't touched it or looked at it in, I don't know, eight years maybe."

"Eight years is a long time."

"And another story. Don't worry about Jake. God made him so he could live on his own without help from man. He'll be fine. You needed the sleep, so I let you. Done chores too. You like sweet-milk pancakes and bacon?"

"I like pancakes and bacon a lot. I don't know about sweet pancakes."

"A sweet-milk is just another pancake, thinner than most, got meat to it though and don't turn to mush after you doctor it like the box stuff does. Got the recipe from an old German friend near fifty years ago. Still use it. I got butter, strawberry preserves, and honey to do the doctoring with. Get your shirt and shoes on and we'll partake."

I didn't have a brain, standing in another man's

house half-dressed. "I'm sorry. I didn't realize." I glanced down at my bare feet and crossed my arms over my chest. "Worried about things I guess."

Back in the room, I pulled up the peach bedspread, straightened the bed and finished dressing. To put my shoes on and tie them, I sat on the edge of a small armchair with a number of stuffed animals. A fuzzy white dog with long ears and only one button eye looked at me over the shoulder of a black teddy bear.

It's funny because I hadn't considered mom. Thoughts of escape always took me into the woods with Cameron and Jake. If I knew where she lived, or had a number to call, then maybe. But she'd given us away because some man said, "It's either me or them two brats. You pick." Why would she want me now? She'd done her choosing.

I gave the stuffed one-eyed dog a scruff and walked to the kitchen.

On the table sat two plates: one with a pancake and two slices of bacon and another with a stack of pancakes an inch thick and half a dozen slices of bacon. He stood at the sink pouring milk into coffee cups. "Take a seat, Ty. I hope I don't have to tell you which one is yours."

He carried the cups over and set one in front of me.

What a great treat. Cold milk in the morning. I remembered my manners and left the fork alone until Ray pulled up his chair.

He'd shaved, didn't look as old, and without the hat, he seemed less menacing. Something still nagged me about him. Either his blue eyes or sharp nose, maybe both, looked like someone I knew.

As soon as he settled in, I picked up the fork but

he bowed his head, something we'd never done at home. The bald spot on top hadn't seen sunlight in awhile.

I lowered my head, but watched his hands lace together on the table.

"Lord, thanks. You done good. Amen." His hands relaxed. "Dig in, son. Honey, preserves, or both. Help yourself to what I've got. The butter is in this little crock. I churn my own. You'll like it. Folks wouldn't need spas if they'd churn their own butter."

The butter spread smooth and melted into little pools on the sweet-milks. I put on a dab of honey then mixed it in.

Ray grabbed the jar. "Watch this. Put it on thick, right down the middle of a sweet-milk." Honey ran out of the jar like it didn't have a thing to do and could take its sweet time. "Then, roll it like you would a newspaper or tortilla. Got to be careful and not let it drip down your front when you eat it. To stop that, fold the bottom end to close it up. Now, take this jar and put on some honey. There's plenty. That drop you smeared around won't go far. Got a tree full of bees back in the woods been providing honey for years."

I tried not to grin, but failed.

Four sweet-milks went down before I thought to breathe. On the last four, I dabbled in the preserves.

Ray poured me another cup of milk, selected a toothpick, and pushed his chair back. "Did you know honey never spoils?" He paused and watched me shovel in the last bite, his mouth opened slightly as mine did, but he didn't wait for me to answer. "Yep, it's the only food source on the planet that lasts forever. It turns to sugar over time and you can eat it like that, but to make it honey again, golden and fluid, all you have to do is heat it up. Leave it to God. Honey, made by Heaven, tastes like Heaven."

A golden drop on the side of my plate drew my finger to it. I wiped it, looked at it, and then licked it off. "Momma Ray made preserves and we had honey, but…" Mr. Ray almost had me talking about what I didn't want to, not yet anyway.

Yes, I'd seen jars of preserves in a rack on the kitchen counter after Momma Ray took them out of the pressure cooker. They disappeared into Dad's bedroom when they cooled.

Ray worked the toothpick a minute, gazing at me. "She did, eh? That your ma?"

"No, sir, I…I ain't seen my real mom for awhile. Might have been in the second grade the last time."

"Son, that's years, not awhile."

The pitcher of milk kept drawing my eyes to it. Ray motioned with his free hand. Another cup would top off the best breakfast I'd eaten for sure. "Yes, sir, it's a long time."

I poured another cup and then held it over Ray's. He declined with a headshake.

"Ty, an old man don't sleep much. I think it's God's way of giving him more time to ponder his life before he dies. Maybe ask Him for the only real gift, forgiveness. My point, last night after you turned in, I sat here thinking. A Don Ray came to mind. He liked to be called D Ray. Had him a young wife and two kids as I recall, but it was some years ago that our paths crossed. I remember him 'cause of his last name: your last name and my first name. Anyway he happen to be your daddy?"

I hesitated and knew I'd just answered the question without opening my mouth. "Yes, sir. That's him."

"And Momma Ray, as you called her, she's your stepmom?"

"Yes, sir."

Ray gathered the plates and carried them to the sink. I followed him and took him by the elbow. "Mr. Ray-Ray, I'll do the dishes. I know soap and water real well."

"All right, I'll let you do that. Soap's under the sink on the right. I got a teapot full of hot water already. Cold is in the bucket in the corner there by the door. Pour a little in each sink and warm it up with the teapot. No use messing with the skillet. I'll wipe it out and put it back with the rest. Washing a seasoned skillet ruins it."

"Yes, sir, I got it. Thanks for breakfast and dinner. The stew tasted good, but I especially liked the sweet-milks."

"Thanks, and you're welcome. I'm going to sit over here and put on my boots. You get done, we'll go see if we can get my pickup cranked and deal with what's on your mind."

He had a way of hinting at a thing without asking.

I poured in the water and soap and gave the plates a good scrubbing. "Mr. Ray-Ray, can I ask you something?"

"Sure, shoot."

"How did you know me and Jake were watching you?"

Ray-Ray finished pulling on a boot, let his foot fall with a thud, then sat up. "You know, I can't answer that right off. I felt something, someone, a look, and from the deepest part of the woods too. A place I'd have never dreamed. 'Course I didn't know it was you, or I wouldn't have taken a pistol with me."

"Mr. Ray-Ray, the pistol didn't bother me none."

"It didn't?"

"No, sir. Not after I looked into your eyes."

Ray nodded. "Well, God's a strange feller. His ways are proof, and He's hard to cipher sometimes. Maybe He set us up. Wanted me to find you and made me aware through my feelings. They say a woman has intuitions about things, and the Lord knows I believe that. My missus could read me like a book. Men have gut feelings. That might be it."

I finished the last dish, placed it in the rack and pulled the rubber stoppers on both sinks. "I can feel my dad looking at me."

Ray finished the second boot and grabbed his hat. "You can feel your dad?"

"Jake knows every time he comes around too."

Ray clapped me on the shoulder. "Come on. Let's get a move on."

His pickup looked a lot like Dad's. Not in color because Ray's was red, but in wear and tear and rust patches in the bottom of the doors and behind each tire.

He opened the driver's door and reached inside. A rapid clicking noise came from under the hood and I knew right off. "The battery's dead Mr. Ray-Ray."

"Yes, sir, you're right as rain, and that's a problem. I have an extension cord, and I have a charger, but I don't think the cord's long enough. We'll check, but I think we'll have to push it closer to the house. Good thing you're here, son. I'd have to lasso Miss May and tie her tail to the bumper."

We shared a chuckle.

A squeak and rattle echoed through the trees. We

turned at the same time and stared down the lane. The car moved like the honey, dodging what had to be limbs, rocks, and potholes on the rough road. Looking from sunlight into shadows made it impossible to see. But then the car passed through a stream of sunlight and revealed a cowboy hat on the dash.

37

Ray pulled off his hat and held it out to shade his eyes from the glare reflected off the windshield. "Hmm, I'll be."

"Sir?" I said.

"I haven't seen this feller in a week."

The white car entered the clearing. As it neared, the little propeller emblem became visible on the hood, and the driver reached and took the hat off the dash and put it on. "Mr. Ray-Ray, that's Mr. Jordan."

"Yep, sure is."

Oh yeah. Dad would be getting his comeuppance now. I'd be going straight to the sheriff.

He stopped.

I stepped to the driver's door, pulled it open, and he stepped out.

"Mr. Jordan..." It's all I could say.

He held me close.

No one spoke.

After a time, I gained control and eased my bear hug from around his chest. He took me by the shoulders, at arm's length.

"Dad went nuts when he seen the apple pie Ed got us at The Burger Stop. I left a shovel handle for whacking his old hog by the door and Dad grabbed it and hit Cameron in the head. Dad had me in mind, but Cameron stepped in and Dad hit him. He's dead. I didn't want to run, but, but—"

"Ty, Ty, wait." Mr. Jordan shook me. "He's not dead, son. Cameron's in the hospital. He has a concussion and a dozen stitches in the side of his head, but he's going to be fine."

A prayer I never prayed, a wish I never wished on a star, had come true, something beyond my wildest imagination, and I didn't believe it. "But, I saw it. Cameron went down, limp as a wet rag. His head exploded, blood everywhere. Dad, he, he chased me out the back door of the barn and something happened and he got Jake with a good lick. I heard him yelp."

"Son." Mr. Jordan bent over with his face close to mine. "Listen, I'm telling you, I talked to Cameron this morning at the hospital. He's as worried about you as you are about him. We're all worried."

"So Cameron's alive. He's OK?"

"He sure is."

We looked at each other, the three of us. They smiled and I know I smiled. My face felt like it had cracks in it. I broke out in a fit of laughter that produced more tears, smiling the whole time.

Then another thought struck me. "Mr. Jordan, I ain't going back to that house, me or Cameron, neither of us. There's no way. We'll both run away. Dad will kill us the next time."

Mr. Jordan's lips pooched out. His cheeks pulled them this way and that way like the words were there, but not in order yet. "Son, your dad is in trouble with the law now. I can't say more. Can you live with that until we get to town?"

A pang of guilt twisted at my stomach. Dad was my dad. Not two minutes ago, I hated him for killing my brother. Now, Cameron's alive, Dad's in trouble, and I'm feeling sorry for him. Then again, if Dad had problems with the law and wound up in jail, we'd be free, me and Cameron. Free of him forever. And we wouldn't be living with Willamina Ray either.

In the end, Dad took care of his own comeuppance. I'm sure glad I didn't drown him.

"Yes, sir, I can wait."

Mr. Jordan stuck his hand out to Ray. "Good morning, big brother."

"Morning, Judge." Ray drew out the title, mocking like, then took the hand and gave it a good shaking.

Mr. Jordan clapped him on the shoulder then put his arm around his neck and kissed him on the bald spot on top of his head. "Better put your hat back on before your head gets sunburned."

Their noses and eyes hit me then. That's where I'd seen it. They had the same look when they pondered how or what to say. Like when Mr. Jordan tried to talk about Randy or tell me about Dad.

Shocked, plum shocked to the bone. What a day.

Ray laughed, put his hat on and gestured at me. "I haven't been able to get a word out of this young man. He's eaten me out of house and home and sweet-milks to boot. You show up, brother, and his gums go to bumping. Now, look at him. A cat's got his tongue. I wish he'd make up his mind."

"I thought I recognized you, Mr. Ray-Ray," I said. "Only I knew we hadn't met. You two look a lot alike now that you're together."

Mr. Jordan took a deep breath and looked over my head toward the house. "We grew up here. Ray is my elder by fifteen years and more than a brother. He raised me after Mom and Dad passed." He gave Ray a playful pat on the belly. "We used to hunt these woods all the way to your house, Ty. Only there wasn't a soul to be seen for miles in those days. We could go plum to town before we crossed a road even.

"Speaking of hunting. Ed and I made a two-mile jaunt across Parson's holler with Ed's dog, yesterday afternoon. We cut a trail that set the dog to baying just before dark, and I knew it had to be you and Jake. That's why I came here this morning. I had my suspicions."

Ray pointed at the car. "You're touring the woods in a luxury car this morning. Where's your pickup? That thing don't like potholes and tree limbs."

"Yes, big brother, you're right about that. Ed got a bad tank of diesel in his pickup and didn't have another fuel filter. He's got mine this morning."

He paused and did a quick scan of the house. "Speaking of hunting, where's Jake? Got him penned?"

My head dropped, chin on my chest. I kicked dirt with a toe. My heart ached. The tears tried to sneak out, but I held them back. "No, sir. He ran off yesterday evening. Let Mr. Ray-Ray sneak up on me and run off. Ain't seen him since."

"I'm sure he'll be fine," Mr. Jordan said. "He'll turn up. And don't you feel bad about letting Ray sneak up on you. He sneaked up on me plenty of times growing up. Let's go see Cameron. You ready? The sheriff's department has a team looking for you too. We need to call them off."

"Ty and I were just about to start pushin' my pickup closer to the house," Ray-Ray broke in. "The battery's dead, and I think it's too far for my extension cord to reach. Better give me a boost before you go."

"I can do that." Mr. Jordan reached through the window, started his car and pulled the hood-latch.

Ray opened the door to his pickup, pulled the

back of the seat forward and grabbed a set of booster cables. They talked as they hooked the two batteries together. "Judge, how's Randy feeling? I've been praying for that boy."

"He's fighting, Ray. Fighting every step."

"Tell him his old unc' will be out to the house in a couple of days, would you?"

"I'll sure do it, Bud. Plan to stay for dinner, if you can stand to eat under electric lights."

Mr. Jordan focused on me and pointed a thumb at his brother. "He put you up in the peach room?"

"Yes, sir," I said. "I woke up this morning and thought where in the world? Kind of expected to see the Mad Hatter."

"So, you're still burning the midnight oil, eh, brother?"

"Long as I'm here by myself, might as well. Ty, that's my granddaughter's room. Amy is growing up fast, so someday I'll have to repaint. Until she tells me, it's peach, peach, and more peach."

"Mr. Ray—"

"She passed away, my missus did. A long time ago."

I kept my trap shut and nodded. I didn't understand the loss of a wife, but I'd lost mom and thought I'd lost Cameron, so the terrible feeling was familiar.

And how did he know what I had in mind to ask him anyway?

The thought of losing Dad didn't hurt and that bothered me.

Mr. Jordan clamped the booster cables on the battery of his car. "Ray, give her a shot and see if it'll start."

The old truck fired and shook like the dickens, running on half its cylinders like Mr. Ray thought it might.

Mr. Jordan removed the cables. "Ray, when you going to get another pickup? I worry about you out here by yourself."

"Ah, this one's good for another hundred thousand miles. No use in wasting money on something I don't use more than once a month."

"I guess. Ty, better give Jake another shout. We need to hit the road. I didn't mention it, but there's someone else waiting to see you besides Cameron."

38

The lane to our house passed on the left, Jason's house on the right. The little white church, its parking area full for Sunday morning services, came and went three miles later. I half expected to see Jake padding up the road or waiting for me at the bus stop like he did on school days.

It felt like a week had passed since Dad's rampage.

Sitting in a car with the windows up revealed a strong odor, and now that I knew its source, it bothered me. "Mr. Jordan, I'm kind of messy to be going into a hospital, or anywhere. My shirt's ripped and dirty, and I smell like I slept with Mr. Ray's hogs last night."

"Well, I'll tell you what. We'll stop at the house right quick and you can clean up. Randy has clothes you can wear. And a pair of shoes too. Yours look like they're about done."

"I'd appreciate that. Momma Ray bought me new shoes for school, but they were too small and hurt my feet."

"Randy's may be too big, but that's better than too small. I'm sure he's got a pair in his closet. We'll see. Are you hungry? I'll stop and get you something if you are."

"No, sir. Mr. Ray-Ray wasn't joshing when he said I ate him out of sweet-milks. I sure had my share and then some, with half a jar of honey. I'm full as a tick."

We weaved our way across town. Not many cars on the road on Sunday mornings. Mr. Jordan had that pondering look I'd seen before, something on his mind.

A ton of things weighed heavy on me and thinking about them hurt. On one hand, no more Dad and living with his ever-present threat. On the other hand, who were we going to live with now? Momma Ray?

"Mr. Jordan, what's next? I mean, for me and Cameron? When he gets out of the hospital, and Dad and Momma Ray…I feel like I'm out of control."

We approached another intersection and the light changed to yellow, then red.

"Ty, right now, I don't know what to tell you. Life hasn't been fair to you and Cameron, and believe it or not, that's a good lesson—one some people never learn."

There wasn't another car in sight, not one on the road but us, like the light knew to turn red and stop us, so we could talk.

He continued. "I think one of the greatest attributes a human can have is a forgiving heart. You have one, and I admire you for it."

Mr. Jordan had a way of making me taller with few words.

The light turned green, but he didn't go. "Ty, do you know Jesus?"

"No, sir. I mean, I read some stories about Him, but I thought He was dead."

"Quite the opposite. He's alive and well, and if you'll ask Him to forgive you of your sins, He'll live in your heart." He patted his chest. "It's called being saved or born again, in spirit."

"You know, no one ever told me about God, not

that I recall, but I've always believed in Him. I know He exists and I know Jesus is His Son."

The light turned green again. Two cars had stacked up behind us. "Then you are truly called, my boy. All you have to do now is ask Him to forgive you and answer the call."

It wasn't hard to see Ray-Ray in Mr. Jordan. They sure had a way with words that set me to thinking.

We pulled in at Mr. Jordan's house and parked in the driveway. "Randy and Karen have gone to church. Come on, you can use Randy's shower. I'll get a towel, anything else you might need, and see if I can find you some duds to wear. I need to call Sheriff Bowles too."

I followed Mr. Jordan down a long hallway, its walls covered in pictures, both on the left and the right. No doubt kinfolk.

One room we passed had a big desk with a leather front and leather chair. Bookshelves full of books covered every wall, floor to ceiling.

Randy's room threw me for a loop. It looked big as our house. Posters of football and baseball players covered the walls. Model cars lined shelves and model airplanes hung from the ceiling from fishing line. Made them look like they were flying around the room. In a corner, next to a sliding glass door that opened out onto a patio, stood a saddle rack with a well-oiled saddle on display.

It was perfect. A blue bedspread printed with brown footballs, without a wrinkle. No shoes, no nothing on the gray carpeted-floor.

Standing in the rain with a bar of soap was one thing, I'd done it, and it didn't take me long to finish my business. Standing in a shower, my first one ever, with hot water pounding me to a beet red, made me want to stay there forever.

Jeans and a green shirt had been left on the bed when I got out. The black tennis shoes he put out for me were too big, but not by much. They'd do to go see my brother.

I'd have to thank Randy the next time we met.

Only the heavy tick of a wall clock could be heard as I wandered back to the entry, then down another long hallway and into the kitchen. The rubber soles on my shoes squeaked on the oak floor in the hall and on the tile in the kitchen.

Mr. Jordan had pulled his car around to the back and had a box he placed in the trunk.

Reading a newspaper had never crossed my mind, and why I glanced at the one on the kitchen table is beyond me. It wasn't the headline, but a little title in a square to one side.

AREA MAN ARRESTED FOR ABUSE

I scanned two short paragraphs looking for a familiar name, down to "See ABUSE A-2", but didn't see one.

The patio door slid open and Mr. Jordan stuck his head in. "You look great, Ty. You ready, then? How was your shower?"

"Yes, sir, I'm ready. Heaven."

"Excuse me."

"Heaven, Mr. Jordan. The shower felt like heaven."

He squeezed my neck and gave me a pat on the back. "Let's go see Cameron."

A Redbone hound ran from the barn to meet me. It was a female, light red and sleek, smaller than a male would be, slight in build. She sniffed me up and down the leg, her tail going ninety miles an hour as I scratched her back.

Mr. Ed came to the door of the barn and yelled for us to wait. He walked with purpose, focused on me, a big smile across his face. Behind him came the cheek-lady from the bait shop.

"Ty," Ed said. "You scared the daylights out of me. Good to see you're safe." He grabbed me in a headlock and rubbed my noggin with a knuckle. "Miss Daisy here cut your track I think. Where'd the Judge find you?"

We shook hands. "At Mr. Ray-Ray's. Sorry for putting you out. I, I never …."

The cheek-lady stood behind Ed, quiet as a mouse, but I knew she'd be grabbing my cheeks or poking me like a melon given the chance.

"Don't be sorry about a thing. Just glad you're here now." He took off his cowboy hat and wiped his forehead. "Ty, this is my wife, Anne Marie."

"Ma'am." A nod was all I could manage.

We hugged and she cupped my face and gave me a kiss on the forehead. She never said a word, not one. Just wiped her eyes and walked back to the barn.

The three of us watched her until she disappeared.

Ed put his hat back on. "Women. Hard to figure sometimes. Old Ray, he's one of a kind. Bet you wondered what in the world you'd walked into when you met him."

"Yes, sir, I sure did."

He gave me another head rub before I got in the car.

Before, the type of attention paid me didn't require my comments. Now, I didn't know what to say or do. I hoped he didn't mind a big smile.

A few things, events, people popping into my life,

our lives, mine and Cameron's, began to make sense.

Mr. Jordan drove us back through town to the hospital. He led me through the reception area and down a long, white-tiled hallway to a nurse's station. Men and women alike, dressed in green tops and pants, worked at different counters and desks.

One of the nurses looked up. Mr. Jordan pointed down another hall. She smiled and waved us on.

I never thought to ask if Cameron was awake or what to expect. The door didn't have a window in it, so not being able to see inside the room added a strong dose of doubt about his condition.

Mr. Jordan gave the door a quick rap with a knuckle, pushed it open, and then stepped aside to let me walk by him.

Cameron was sitting up in bed dressed in a white undershirt and what looked like blue gym shorts. Other than a white bandage around his head, he looked great, smiling.

A tall lady stood next to him pouring water into a plastic cup. She had shoulder length brown hair pulled behind her ears, and she wore a white blouse and tan slacks. She glanced up and placed the pitcher on the cart next to Cameron.

To my right, a man leaned against the windowsill. A serious looking man, or at least his short hair and big arms made him look like he meant business. Just to his left, on the sink, lay a blue motorcycle helmet with a white star on the side of it.

We exchanged looks, the four of us, left, right, right, left. Tears streamed from the lady's eyes.

My throat caught just in time to keep my heart from jumping out of my chest onto the foot of Cameron's bed. "Mom?"

39

Sitting in the chair next to Cameron, listening to Mom and John T.—the private investigator she'd hired to check on us—I remembered the story Brother Mark told us in church about Joseph and his brothers.

…and he fell upon his brother Benjamin's neck, and wept; and Benjamin wept upon his neck.

Moreover he kissed…

It was sure good to see Cameron.

John T. hopped onto the edge of the sink. "Anyway, I hit the kill switch, coasted the last hundred yards and pulled off the road. I tried to be quiet as possible even though I was still a ways from the house. I knew your dog would be there about the time I got my helmet off. I gave him two dog biscuits, then here came a truck. That was no big deal. All I had to do was be still and wait for it to pass. Then you two yahoos took off running so close to me I nearly had a heart attack. I didn't have a clue you were there."

Cameron choked back laughter and wiped tears from his eyes. "Yeah, and I heard you whack something."

John T. threw his arms out, palms up. His voice went up a note. "I ran into a tree. Almost broke my neck. I saw the trunk, but missed seeing the big limb. It got me across the chest." He made a motion from shoulder to shoulder. "I waited ten minutes or so then sneaked in to watch the house. When I got back to my bike and my helmet was gone, that really threw me. I actually felt my head thinking I'd forgot to take it off. It took me a little while to find it, digging around in the dark in that old barn. I expected to have a rat trap take a bite of a finger, or some animal to attack me every time I reached under something."

"Wait, wait," I said, "Cameron, how, how did you get away? How'd you get here?"

Cameron pointed to John T.

John T. answered for him. "I'd just parked the bike and made a circle through the woods to the back of the barn when your dad came home. Ty, you nearly ran right over me when he chased you from the barn. Your dog tripped him up and just in time too, because he about had you."

"Did Jake bite him? I heard Dad hit heavy and yell."

"Yep, your dog bit him, and he fell on a pile of boards full of nails and suffered a puncture wound to the right forearm."

Cameron shook his head. "Set his own trap. He's the one who insisted on stacking them boards there. Then he ran over them."

John T. gestured to Cameron and mom. He opened his mouth to talk and then closed it.

Mom said, "John, just tell them. There's no love lost."

"I suppose," he said. "Just didn't want to tell your story."

"Just tell it. They're already men. Didn't get a chance to be kids. They can handle it, and I don't need to tell it."

"I made a citizen's arrest you might say. I suppose your dad can file on me for trespassing, but I don't care. I didn't see him hit Cameron, but I heard it, all of it, and I saw him leave the barn, after you, wielding the shovel handle. I had to hold him at gunpoint. Your stepmom called the police."

"Momma Ray called the police on Dad? Hard to believe she'd ever do something like that," I said.

"I made her. I didn't know if Cameron would live or die, and I couldn't turn my back on your dad. I forced him to carry Cameron into the house. Then he got to sit on his hands on the living room floor until the ambulance and police arrived. There's a lot of hate in that guy. Sheriff Bowles hauled him to jail. He's been charged with child abuse and assault, just two that I know of. The judge set bail at five hundred grand. He'll have to come up with ten percent to get out."

"Which judge? Mr. Jordan?" I said.

John T. nodded.

It took me a second to do the ciphering. No way Dad would get out of jail, not unless he could get someone to buy his junky old haying equipment. Even that might not be enough.

Cameron shifted around on the bed. "The other day, Dad and Momma Ray ran off to town on an errand, or so they said. They came back acting like someone had given them what for. Momma Ray had a bunch of papers under her arm. You have something to do with that, Mom?"

"Their errand was breakfast. My lawyer met them at the restaurant and served them with papers. I'm suing for custody."

"Mom, what…" I didn't mean to be so obvious in front of John T., but questions he didn't need to hear burned on my tongue.

Mom must have known. All she had to do was

glance at him and he picked up his helmet and walked to the door. "I'm going to get a cup of coffee, Mrs. Brooks. You need me, I'll be in the cafeteria."

"Thanks, John."

"Wait," I said. "One more question. Why the motorcycle?"

"You live too far back in the woods. Nowhere to park a car out of sight. Even the bike was a chore without a headlight to see where I was going. You probably didn't see it, but I put a little strip of reflective tape on a tree about two hundred yards from where I parked, so I'd know where to shut the lights off."

He stood there a moment with the helmet under his arm. "Well, if you need me, you know where I'm at. Glad you're safe." He gave a quick salute and disappeared down the hallway.

Mom looked like...well, I don't know what. I remembered turmoil. Early mornings, ragged hair, red eyes, screaming for us to be quiet so she could sleep. Different men in our lives. Some who liked kids and some who didn't, mostly the latter.

The woman staring at me now didn't look like the mom I remembered. Her blouse and pants, her attitude, and the way she carried herself didn't fit the image I had stored away.

"Mom. Mrs. Brooks?"

"I'm remarried, Ty. His name is James, James Brooks. He's a great guy, and I love him. We live in Houston, Texas—where you'll be living soon."

"Where have you been? How come you haven't been to see us? When was the last time?"

Cameron puffed up a little. "Hey, she had an order."

"Cameron, I bet you had your questions

answered," I puffed back. "She's my mom too. You just sit there and be quiet."

Mom walked to the armchair and sat down. "I wasn't fit to be a mom. Son, I'm sorry. I was really messed up for a long time. All I can tell you is, I'm sorry and I love you. Do you forgive me?"

We met at the foot of the bed and cried.

I guess Cameron had already done his crying, so he sat and kept his tongue.

Mom and I turned loose of each other when a nurse walked in. The lady had a great smile, one that made you want to be near her. She fussed over Cameron, and I would have sworn Cameron looked like he got sicker as she checked the bandage and used a small light to look into his eyes. Big faker was wallowing in the attention of a pretty girl.

I couldn't help myself. "Ma'am, did, did you see anything in there?"

She gave me a quick look. She must have realized what I meant. "The back of his head is all." She pinched Cameron's cheek. "We're going to let you get out of here before lunch, young man. Doctor Lowery will be in. He's making his rounds right now. As soon as he sees you, I'm sure you'll be free to go. Course, I'll have to wheel you out. We don't let patients walk out of here these days. Any questions?"

Mom spoke. "I think there's some paperwork I need to take care of."

"Yes, you can stop downstairs at Admissions on the way out. Of course, if you don't want to sign, we can keep him here and put him to work changing bedpans and such." Her green eyes lit.

Cameron's face wrinkled up like an old pug dog. We both had to think about that a minute, then we let out an "eww" at the same time.

The nurse shook her head once and gave mom a sideways glance. "Sounds like you better make sure you take him with you. He won't be much use around here if he won't change a bedpan."

Mom put one hand on Cameron's leg and grabbed me around the neck and squeezed. "I'm going to take them both."

I put an arm around her and squeezed back. "You mean that? We're going with you?"

"It seems you two have a special friend in Judge Jordan. He's already signed the papers."

Oh yeah. Me and Cameron slapped hands.

Doctor Lowery showed up and gave Cameron and Mom a lecture about contact sports. Cameron's concussion, his condition, couldn't take the beating on a football field. I wanted to say something smart about Dad and his right hook, but thought better of it.

Mom assured him Cameron would not hit nor be hit anytime soon.

The nurse with the pretty smile arrived with a wheelchair as the doc left, loaded Cameron up, and pushed him down the hall and out the front door.

Mom pulled to the curb in a red Saab. "Boys, we're staying in a hotel tonight, out on the Interstate. Tomorrow, well, tomorrow we'll think more about what's next. We have years to make up for."

Mom had a bunch of stuff on the front seat, so I opened the back door for Cameron. "Mom, you heard us talk about my dog, Jake. I can't leave him here."

She looked down and scanned her car and its tan leather seats. I know she was thinking there's no way a dog is riding in my car, but she smiled and her eyes softened. "Where is he? We'll pick him up and take him with us."

Cameron had a questioning look on his face.

I shrugged.

"Ty, did Jake run off?"

Tears welled up. "He left me yesterday, at Ray's house. Ain't seen him since." I don't know how I uttered the words. I got in next to Cameron and closed the door. All at once, the world didn't look the same anymore. It was like waking up from a dream.

Mom kept an eye on us in the rearview mirror as she drove through town. I could see light in those blue eyes, and the light sparked something in me I'd not felt in a long time—hope.

If Cameron didn't wipe the smile off his face, it was going to stay that way.

Mom braked for a light, one of the last lights before we reached the big highway, the one down to Little Rock.

On the side street to my right stood a small boy of maybe ten or twelve years of age. Not much younger than me and Cameron. A little blonde-headed girl in a dirty yellow dress stood next to him holding his hand. Next to her was my friend, Jake. He sat on his haunches, still as a statue. She put her hand on him. His tail wagged the second she touched him. He looked at her, stared at her. She gave him a pat and scratched his head. The hand seemed detached, loving and patting Jake on its own, as she scanned the street left and right.

I wanted to yell out to Jake, to Mom and Cameron, to the kids with Jake. I wanted to tell them, "that's my dog, my friend, and I want him back." But I sat there like a bump on a pickle.

An old white pickup stopped at the curb in front

of the kids. The boy walked to the back and lowered the tailgate. Jake jumped but didn't make it all the way in, his back legs hanging. The boy helped him and closed the tailgate.

The little girl managed to open the passenger's door, but the boy said something that caused her to stop. Her shoulders jerked as the lady driving the pickup gestured and leaned toward her. I didn't hear, but the girl's reactions were enough.

She put a foot in the doorway, but the boy stopped her and got in first. He helped the girl, then reached across her and pulled the door shut.

Cameron and I had our noses pressed to the window. The knot in my throat wasn't something I could swallow.

Cameron whispered, "You got to let him go, Bud. They need him now. Got to let an angel do his work." He gave my shoulder a squeeze and sat back in the seat.

The light turned green.

THE BEGINNING

About the Author

Boo Riley (also known as David Arp) was born in 1957 in Safford, Arizona. He spent his youth in Lubbock, Texas, where he started working the oilfields as a roughneck soon after graduating from high school. Today, though he lives in Colorado, he travels the world employed as a drilling supervisor. He loves to write.

Thank you…

for purchasing this Watershed Books title. For other inspirational stories, please visit our on-line bookstore at www.pelicanbookgroup.com.

For questions or more information, contact us at customer@pelicanbookgroup.com.

Watershed Books
Make a Splash!™
an imprint of Pelican Book Group
www.PelicanBookGroup.com

Connect with Us
www.facebook.com/Pelicanbookgroup
www.twitter.com/pelicanbookgrp

To receive news and specials, subscribe to our bulletin
http://pelink.us/bulletin

May God's glory shine through
this inspirational work of fiction.

AMDG

You Can Help!

At Pelican Book Group it is our mission to entertain readers with fiction that uplifts the Gospel. It is our privilege to spend time with you awhile as you read our stories.

We believe you can help us to bring Christ into the lives of people across the globe. And you don't have to open your wallet or even leave your house!

Here are 3 simple things you can do to help us bring illuminating fiction™ to people everywhere.

1) If you enjoyed this book, write a positive review. Post it at online retailers and websites where readers gather. And share your review with us at reviews@pelicanbookgroup.com (this does give us permission to reprint your review in whole or in part.)

2) If you enjoyed this book, recommend it to a friend in person, at a book club or on social media.

3) If you have suggestions on how we can improve or expand our selection, let us know. We value your opinion. Use the contact form on our web site or e-mail us at customer@pelicanbookgroup.com

God Can Help!

Are you in need? The Almighty can do great things for you. Holy is His Name! He has mercy in every generation. He can lift up the lowly and accomplish all things. Reach out today.

Do not fear: I am with you; do not be anxious: I am your God. I will strengthen you, I will help you, I will uphold you with my victorious right hand.
~Isaiah 41:10 (NAB)

We pray daily, and we especially pray for everyone connected to Pelican Book Group—that includes you! If you have a specific need, we welcome the opportunity to pray for you. Share your needs or praise reports at http://pelink.us/pray4us

Free Book Offer

We're looking for booklovers like you to partner with
us! Join our team of influencers today and periodically
receive free eBooks and exclusive offers.

For more information
Visit http://pelicanbookgroup.com/booklovers